ANGELO LOUKAKIS

VERNACULAR DREAMS

To Ann with Love

CONTENTS

I sit outside the theatre and can do nothing but exercise my memory. As I wait to see if he will live (they tell me this open-heart stuff has a ninety-five per cent success rate), I make him young again. I find him in another life. The late fifties, early sixties, they were his salad days.

Say Christmas around 1960.

My memory lets me down on this, but, on the theory that there were always heatwaves in our little Arncliffe, I would say this was a week of heat. Why not? I can remember nearly everything else.

He comes up from the yard behind the shop, in his singlet. It's soaked in sweat.

'We can do nothing about this heat. We have to live with it. Open the doors, close the doors, what's the difference? We are baking in hell.'

'Doesn't matter,' I say. 'Christmas is soon. Aren't we gonna put up decorations? All the big shops have decorations, why can't we have some?'

'*Kala. Pare* six bob from the till. Six bob only. Go up the paper shop. But listen, don't bring me back rubbish.'

I take at least eight bob and go via Frank's Milk Bar so I can play the pinball first. The Hawaii machine, two games for one shilling, replay for lucky number. And only then do I go, two doors up, to the paper shop and buy glass baubles and tinsel and a cardboard Santa. Mrs Mack wraps it up in brown paper, and after that, I start back to our Mixed Business.

I always hate the bits of footpath with no awnings in the summer because it's always so stinking hot. And so I run the last little bit to our place, and finish up red and panting anyway. But I have to get inside quick, don't I?

He doesn't look in the parcel straight away. He always thinks I never do as I'm told. So he just asks, and I tell him what I got. He doesn't say anything else, so I must have done right, probably ...

'But still we have to get the trees don't forget,' I say.

'Tomorrow.'

The sister comes and calls me, because they are wheeling him out of the operating theatre and into intensive care. How is he? Reasonable. It was a bit complicated. A couple of things the surgeon wasn't expecting. He is stable, however.

When I see him, he doesn't recognize me. He is doped up and will remain that way for a couple more days, they tell me.

The next day when I come to visit he is asleep, and I wait in a chair by his bed. Where was I? I was going to go to the markets today, to buy the trees.

I had this pet thermometer which I bought at the

chemist and carried around with me everywhere. No doubt I had it in my pocket that December morning.

I do up the button on my shirt pocket so it doesn't fall out when we push the Renno around the corner. I help him do this every day so it can roll down the hill and get started. There's something wrong with the battery. There's always something wrong with the battery.

And it's hot again today. In the car, I look at the temperature on my thermometer. Eighty degrees at nine a.m.

I love it at the markets, the Haymarket, the way he knows everybody, their names, and everybody knows him.

'We go to the Chinese man for Christmas trees, but first we got to get fruit and vegetables,' he says. He sends me to get a trolley. Then he lets me wheel it to the first stand, and then it starts to get full, and then he takes over.

A box of lettuce, a box of tomatoes, a half-case of cucumbers, a sack of onions ...

'Enough until after Christmas,' he says. I know we don't sell much. He pushes all the stuff back to the car and I help him put it in. I watch the muscles move on his arms. He's got big hands too. (I look at mine and compare them to his as he lies there, still groggy, twenty-four hours after they slit his chest open. His hands are still large. Mine are still small. Except for them, every part of him seems wired to something, and there are drips in his forearms.)

Then he says—

'Go to the Chinese man, you know the one, and wait. I'll be there in a minute for the trees.'

I know what he does. When he sends me to wait somewhere at the markets, it's so he can go to one of the pubs and have a couple of quick ones. I don't care. Only I'm not supposed to tell my mother what he does, he told me once.

When he comes back, he's smiling at me, looking like it's *him* that's done something wrong for a change. But not really wrong, and we're both in it together, aren't we? He kisses me, even though he knows I don't like him doing it when anybody is around.

And now, twenty years later, he's lying in this hospital bed. He's been coming round for the last hour or two. Finally, he moves his arm, meaning that I should come closer.

'What time it is?'

'Two in the afternoon.'

'I woke up so quick,' he says slowly.

He is thinking it is the afternoon of the day of his operation.

'It's not the same day. It's two o'clock the next day. It's Wednesday today,' I tell him. He nods and then closes his eyes again. He seems so incredibly tired. I stay a little longer, then leave to go back to the office.

Today, three days after his operation, they tell me he is going to be alright. I settle back to pass the time while he sleeps, playing my game, putting it all back together again. There was a time when he wasn't such a mess. I wish it were still here, that time.

Mr Chin starts up like he always does—

'Is he a good boy?'

'Yes, he's a good boy,' my father answers.

'Help his father?'

'Yes, he help his father.'

Mr Chin smiles at me.

'Help your father, son. Jackie here works hard. I work bloody hard myself.'

Mr Chin calls everyone Jackie. My father's name is Pavlos. 'Help your father son,' I keep thinking as he picks out three small trees. I take out my thermometer as we head back to the car. Ninety today. How are we gonna get the trees in the car? The ends will have to stick out the window, he says.

We pull them out of the car first when we get back. One is for us, one is for Mrs Riley, and one is to put in the shop for sale—only one because our customers usually get their trees from the big fruit and veg. up the road.

Christmas Eve? I would have delivered the tree that was ordered, like I always did. My father puts our own tree in an old five-gallon ice-cream tin with some water, and carries it into our living room behind the shop. He puts some Christmas paper around the tin to hide it. Then I'm allowed to put the decorations up.

Christmas morning 1960? Presents. Some clothes, a model airplane kit from Phil, son of the lady who cleans the shop once a week. And I get a Meccano set from my parents. This part I like. But then my father says Kosta and Maria and Dimitri and some other friends of my mother's are going to come around in the afternoon— same as every Christmas. They'll make Greek food, which I like, but they'll play records on the radiogram too, which I don't. Her records are always whining ones, and everyone is always singing high notes. And that's how it was.

And I'm thinking maybe after lunch I'll remind him of those times. He likes to hear stories about the past, not much less than he likes telling them.

I watch him eat, slowly cutting up his cottage pie and piling small amounts of potato onto his fork. I know he doesn't like this sort of food. He likes plenty of salsa, lamb and beans done Greek style, everything juicy. He pushes the bowl of custard with half an apricot on top to one side. He does like tea, however, which he eventually drinks leaning back against the pillows.

'Almost Christmas ... Are you feeling sentimental?' I ask him.

An ironic smile, and he points to the dressing on his chest.

'Here is my present,' he shakes his head, and then tears well in his eyes.

'I've been thinking of Christmas when I was a kid ... Do you remember when I was always at you to buy the decorations? And I came to the markets to buy trees? Remember? Every year I used to ...'

'Not *every* year,' he says. 'You come a couple of times.'

'I used to deliver them to your customers.'

'Sometimes ...' He smiles again. 'You didn't like to make the deliveries. You complained. I want to go out! I want to ride my bike! ... You forget.'

'Remember the trouble we used to have with those old Rennos? Trying to get them started to go to the markets?'

He grins again. 'The Renno was a good car.'

'That's not what I thought,' I say, knowing that when he interrupts me like this, I may as well give up. He's not in his listening mood. Anything you say he just takes as a cue for himself.

'The doctors say everything is OK, you are going to be alright.'

I hold his hand but he doesn't seem to notice. He seems to drift off for a few moments, then he says—

'Yes. The surgeon come to see me before. Same thing, he said.'

'It's a pity you won't be out for Christmas.'

'Pah. I don't care about Christmas. You know that.'

'Not even if you were in Greece?' I say, trying to get him onto his favourite subject.

My old man lives in his mind, and always, for as long as I've been aware of these things, has done. It's the only way he can cope with his life, which he hasn't liked for years, but hasn't been able or willing to fix either. In recent years I've spent plenty of energy trying to find things we could talk to each other about—although he himself has never bothered to do the same. I haven't been able to find too many. My father is a very selfish man.

'If I had stayed in Greece, I never would be sick. In Australia everybody gets sick, doctors, hospital all the time.'

'It's the change of diet. Too much animal fat. No exercise. Too much stress. All those things have ...'

'No, it's the water,' he says. 'And the climate. All my life here, forty years, I never had a drink of water taste good. Clean water. From the mountains, and cold. I remember still the taste ... You telling me before about Christmas when you was a kid. When I was young, not just twenty, but *fifty* years before, I can remember, and I can tell you.'

'So tell me.'

'We had plenty holidays. St Nicholas Day and Christmas and New Year and *Ta Fota*. We play cards, everybody get together and we play cards on the eve of New Year—*ti Kali Hera*, we call it. In winter don't forget, I'm talking about. In the village we kill one or two pigs and make sausages. Only one time a year we had sausages. That was Christmas time. And the smell, and the taste, mmm ...'

'Did it snow where you were?'

'Yes, sometimes it snow too.'

The nurse comes to take pulse and blood pressure readings, and while she's doing that I go for a walk down the corridor.

I am so tired of humouring him, even as sick as he has been. I've humoured him for years, and I'm doing it now. I wonder when it's going to end. Probably never.

I've been looking after him for years, although he doesn't seem to realize, or want to acknowledge the fact. I've arranged for this operation. I'm paying his bills. And what's my return? Nil. He doesn't really care about me.

He switched off years ago. When he decided that fate had dealt him blows he just hadn't deserved, he cut everyone out. My mother, myself, everyone. He couldn't cope, so he made life a misery for everyone else.

As I walk back towards his part of the ward, I see the nurse exit.

'How are they, Mr Krinos's readings?'

'They're fine. He's doing well.'

When I get to his bed he says—

'You didn't go. I thought maybe you go back to work.'

'No I'm still here.'

'I remember some more. You talk before about Christmas, what you did. And I tell you about snow in the old country?'

'Yes.'

'I remember something more ... One time, near Christmas, or end of the year—I'm talking maybe 1927, '28—my father tell me he have a job for me—to take some potatoes, a sack of potatoes he grow himself, to my uncle up in Varvisa. Varvisa is the village high up from us in the mountains. I was twelve, thirteen *chronos*. I never been to that place by myself before—but I know where it is. That's what I say to myself. The donkey I been riding everywhere else, so my father say, take the donkey, put the potatoes in the pack, and take him up to Varvisa.

'It was afternoon when he tell me to do this job. Really, it takes one day to go up to Varvisa and come back down. He gives me only half-day. But I love my father and I do what he say. I take the donkey and start to go to my uncle in Varvisa.

'The road is very long. Ten kilometres. Twelve kilometres, maybe more. And ...'

He can't find the word, and tilts his hand upwards instead.

'Steep,' I say.

'Steep. Yes. Steep ... Only times before I went to this village I went with my father. And this time I think to myself, I know how to go there. So, I'm going. One hour. Two hour. Should be about three hour. But three hour pass and no *horio*, no Varvisa. Then four hour. It's after four o'clock. It's late. Then I see I am lost. I am lost. I have to think what to do. What can I do? I turn around and come back down.

'And I am very upset. All the way I come back down I think how stupid I am, how every time I do wrong thing. My father send me to do the job, like man, and I can't do it.

'Anyway, I am back in Ritopolis, oh, after dark, and I put the donkey in the shed, and quietly I take potatoes and pack off him. I am doing this and my father hear the noise and he come to the shed. He has the lamp with him, because it is dark in there, and he see me. Me and the potatoes.'

'What did you say?'

'I say nothing. I am very upset. I remember even now. I start to cry. He say to me "I send you to do job, to your uncle, and you come back like this. What's the matter with you? Where you been?" He ask me questions and questions, and me, I am crying.'

And my old man's eyes, which had been welling up as he was speaking, finally spill over.

'It's alright,' I say to him, 'It's alright. That was a long time ago. It's all over now. All over. Come on. You're alright.'

I take his hand, and the tears start to subside.

'You've been through a lot,' I say. 'The operation was hard, I know. But you're going to be better now.'

He nods hopefully. He just nods. Looking like the kid he really is. And immediately succeeds in turning me off again. He is so self-indulgent it is unbelievable. How I am going to put up with his old age is beyond me. There's no-one else to look after him. He's only in his sixties and already he's a fond old fool. I don't know what the answer is. I know I can't go on resenting him like this, I'll finish up with some disease myself.

I think there's nothing I can do but just put up with it. Depressing as that prospect is. I decide I should leave him for today.

'I'm going now,' I try to tell him, but he's so tired, he's already falling asleep. A meal and fifteen minutes' talk is enough to wipe him out at this stage of his recovery.

I walk away from the ward. The answer is to try not to think what things might be like tomorrow. Being here now is what I should be aiming at. Great.

HOORAY FOR HARALAMBOS

From his position behind the counter in the Trousers Department, Neil's main view was of Suits. For someone who had never owned one, it had been a tempting view. So much so that last week, on one of his periodic glides down to that section, he had succumbed, and chosen the outfit he was now wearing.

The Suit Department was his first destination this morning. He wanted to see if any more in his style had been sold, if anyone else had vindicated his taste. He had bought this three-piece, dark blue, pinstriped number last Friday, with his first pay from Brewers. He had landed a job here as a 'trainee executive', his eighth job in six years, and the best-paying so far; enough for a suit, and bus and lunch money for two weeks, all out of a single pay packet.

He went through the rack and found the two other sizes, same as last week. It pleased him in a kind of way, being the only guy around in a suit like this.

He glanced in the direction of the office behind the racks every so often, in case any of the bosses spotted him. The bosses he had become aware of so far were the assistant buyer Hats, the buyer Suits and Trousers, and the floor manager—shits one and all. Not wanting to push his luck too far, he slid back to Trousers before two minutes were up.

He wasn't afraid of them, of being reprimanded, or anything like that. He just didn't like having to explain or give an account of himself—especially to people in authority. When put on the spot, in situations where power seemed to him to be unjustly apportioned, he invariably became angry, and sometimes flushed. He had learned, however, to preempt such problems by way of a strategic retreat.

With custom as slow as it was today, he began to look for things to do to pass the time. He busied himself for a while restocking one of the trouser bars. That done, he thought he should take a look at the handouts he had been given at last week's training session, seeing he was meant to go to classes again later in the morning.

He took his case out from where he kept it beneath the counter, and removed a bundle of papers. These he placed on top of the counter so he could leaf through them. A 'trainee executive' indeed. It really was a dopey proposition.

About a month earlier, when he had tried to explain to his parents that a trainee executive was really only a sales assistant who had to go to classes, his father had dismissed it all with a wave of his calloused hand. *He* knew what an executive was—an executive is a boss. There were plenty of the same in the paint factory where he worked. They lived in a glass office over the factory floor, he had told him. Nor was the old man impressed when told that buyers and floor managers—which is what you eventually became—were very highly paid. So what, garbage men are very highly paid too, he had said.

Neil took the Company's Pledge To Our Customers and began to read. At the top of the list of promises was the declaration that the first duty of the staff of Brewers Pty Ltd was to its customers. The Customer, it said, Is King. He tried to recall whether he had seen this pledge on display anywhere around the store, but was convinced it wasn't. It was a load of horseshit as far as he was concerned. Like much of the rest of the stuff he was supposed to read for this week.

When one of the dowagers from Hats behind the escalators came to relieve him at eleven, he went off to class. The correct frame of mind was lacking however. Last week's session had consisted of two hours on Modern Merchandising, and two hours on Understanding Profit. As much as he liked wearing a suit as opposed to overalls or dustcoats, he wasn't sure he could believe in buying and selling as a way of life.

Going up in the lift he had flashes of the job before this one. Christmas and New Year in the paint factory. When the Christmas rush petered out, they had sacked him from his temporary Australia Post thing, leaving him short of money at a bad time. But his old man had come to the rescue. A storeman's offsider for three months. Great.

He took a seat in a row towards the back of the lecture room, then watched as the other trainees entered in ones and twos. They all seemed so bright-eyed and bushy-tailed it was unreal. He wished he too could believe in things the way some of these trainees—who were mostly five or six years younger than him—seemed to believe in what they were doing.

A freckle-faced man with red hair, about his own age, came in and went to the lectern at the front. He put his papers down and before anyone had been able to settle he began—

'A role play today, folks, to start with. The situation is this ...'

Mr Andrews, training officer, went on to describe what he called a 'typical example of poor customer relations'. He would take the part of a sloppy assistant if someone would play the part of a customer ... And on he went.

It didn't take Neil too long to switch off. He leaned over to his case and pulled out a magazine, a copy of *Time*, to which he had recently become a subscriber. He spread it out on his lap and searched the contents page for something interesting. It caused him trouble in parts, referring to people and events he couldn't honestly say were ever much on his agenda—current affairs had never been his best subject. But he saw the magazine as important. If nothing else, buying it and reading it was an expression of a desire to acquire some new ideas; more than that, to help him answer the question of what to do with himself. With what was called work, he had hit a dead end.

He was in the doorway of the lunchroom waiting to enter when he saw Andrews beckon to him from further along the passageway. He went to him, thinking that maybe he had been caught not paying attention earlier.

'Manopoulos, isn't it?'

'Yes.'

'Neil Manopoulos? ... Right ... I was asked to tell you to report to Personnel.'

He felt he was about to have a panic attack, until Andrews grinned.

'It's OK. I think they're going to give you an assignment. They like to shift the trainees around to different areas. Give youse a broader experience of the operation, you know. So, two o'clock, see Mr Penshurst.'

'Mr Manopoulos, we have an assignment for you which I hope will please. It should. Not many of the trainees get something like this in their first year ... Now, have you heard of Claudio Panatto?'

Penshurst saved him the trouble of saying no.

'Of course, everyone has. We're lucky enough to be having him in Australia next week to do a series of promotions. In fact, we'll be opening a boutique within this store to carry his fashions. As you can imagine, it's a bit of a coup ... But what we want you to do is to act as a kind of liaison officer for us.'

'Liaison.'

'That's right. What we want is for you to look after his hotel bookings, make sure he's got a hire car when he wants one, that sort of thing. Pick him up and bring him here for photo sessions. Any special needs he might have. Whatever's necessary ... Do you think you could handle that?'

How Neil wanted to respond was with a 'no'. Instead, he looked at his shoes and began to think of what more than 'yes' or 'OK' he could say. In the end he opted for 'yes, I think so'.

'Of course you can. It's a challenge isn't it? We want to encourage responsibility in our trainee managers, and I've been told you're one of the more promising ones ... Oh, and I don't think you should be worried about Mr Panatto. He's charming, charming. I've met him of course. Your own foreign background should stand you in good stead here. You should be able to relate to Mr Panatto, make him feel at home, I would say probably better than most.'

The 'foreign' stuff always made him squirm, but Neil wondered more about who it was that said he was 'promising'. One thing he didn't want was to be promising, or responsible. For $150 a week he wanted the minimum of hassle.

'An added bonus for you,' Penshurst said, suddenly producing a leer, 'is he's bringing a couple of models with him. European girls I've heard. You should like that.'

During the next few evenings Neil took a number of phone calls at home on the matter of Claudio Panatto. Most of them were from people in Ladies' Fashions who had thought up wonderful promotional stunts and who wanted to make sure that Neil would deliver Panatto to wherever they were meant to happen. These calls, which sometimes came as late as eleven p.m., were none too well received by his father.

Picking up what must have been the sixth or seventh, he went right off and shouted 'Bloody another one!' down the hall.

Neil came out of his room to see his father holding the receiver at arm's length, as if it were a smelly fish— naturally he hadn't bothered to cover the mouthpiece.

After handing it to him, he took a couple of steps backwards. He stood there and watched quietly, knowing this annoyed his son, but determined to find out what was happening.

His son had become very close about this new job of his. 'Yes, spot on ... sounds great ...' he heard him say over and over. He had this habit of always making his voice sound different when he spoke on the phone, more Australian—and older, like he was trying to act older than his twenty-two years.

In the end, he put the phone down and went away without explaining anything. He had picked up some very bad habits, this boy of his. It was very hard to understand why he refused to explain anything to him any more.

Of the sights on the way to the airport, where they were supposed to meet Panatto, Neil saw nothing. He had been trying to cope with too many stimuli as it was. He had sat next to one of Brewers' directors, the company's special projects man, for one thing. For another, it was the first time he had ridden in a Rolls Royce. He had become agitated trying to make conversation and his face was flushed.

They stood for over an hour in the reception area waiting for Panatto to appear. Neil still felt red. He was about to go to the Men's to throw some water on his face when Fielding suddenly took the cigarillo he had been smoking out of his mouth and jabbed him in the arm.

'There they are.'

Neil stared at the gate, but didn't really know who to look for.

'Over there,' Fielding pointed him out, 'with the black girl.'

There was another woman with Panatto, tall, with cropped blonde hair, but it was the black girl who caught the eye of the obese and greying director, as she did Neil's. Didn't Penshurst say they were going to be European? Fielding waved frantically in Panatto's direction until Panatto saw him. He came over, smiling slyly, to join them.

Fielding and Panatto exchanged greetings, the girls standing grimly in the background. Neil was unprepared for these arrivals. The girls were so tall, much taller than himself, and looked stunning. Panatto himself was tall and slim, his silvery hair a mass of neat waves. The English he spoke so softly was impeccable. Neil had been expecting an Italian.

'And I'd like you to meet Neil Manopoulos, Claudio.'
Panatto gently extended his hand.

'Neil will be looking after you and Barbara and Adriana while you're here.'

On hearing their names the girls came to life, both edging forward together and smiling their dazzling smiles. Neil nodded to them in a way he hoped was not too uncool, and eventually touched each of their hands.

Again, this time on the way to Panatto's hotel, Neil found it difficult to place himself. He was all the way conscious of the variety of bodies now cramped into the car, of the cold air coming from the air-conditioning, and of the oppressive perfume—Panatto's own brand—which was everywhere.

They made a brief stop at the main store to deposit Fielding, before the final few kilometres to William Street. When he saw they were approaching the hotel, Neil took a number of deep breaths, as furtively as possible. In the entrance drive, a doorman approached, and for the first time ever someone helped him exit a car door. But he got out smiling. The only way he was going to cope with all this was to pretend that he had always lived this life.

Panatto stayed in the foyer while Neil helped the two models carry their hand luggage up to their suite—for some reason it surprised him to find they were sharing rooms with Panatto.

Inside, as they fussed about dropping bags and opening wardrobe doors, Neil occasionally got a close-up of one or the other of this pair. He was fascinated by the black one, who turned out to have an American accent. Were they still called negresses, he wondered? It didn't sound right. She had the most amazingly beautiful skin, smooth as he didn't know what. Black. No. Just non-white.

He was trying the TV to see if it worked when it came to him—the answer to the problem of how you describe people without using labels. You didn't. He hardly had time to be pleased with himself for this, the first original thought he'd had in days, when the person who'd inspired it suddenly slammed the door of the bar fridge. She turned to face Neil, her hands on her hips.

'Neil, right?'

'Yes, and you're ...', to his disgrace he couldn't remember her name. Rather, he couldn't remember which one was which.

'Barbara. How about ringin' for some juice. There's none here I can find.'

'Righto.'

He lifted the phone to dial room service. As he dialled, Adriana exited the bathroom carrying her make-up bag. She was wearing only panties. She emptied the contents of the bag on the benchtop next to the phone and spread them all around, leaned forward and began looking for something. How could she act as if he wasn't standing there right next to her? He wished he could be as totally indifferent as she so obviously was.

'Fuck it!' she said, when she couldn't find what she was looking for. Neil didn't know whether turning the other way was enough. It crossed his mind to make a discreet move for the door, but he decided to stay with it. So, with his face to the wall he ordered, as calmly as he could manage, a jug of orange juice.

On Tuesday and Wednesday Neil left his home in Dulwich Hill in his new suit and arrived at the hotel, always only just in time, to ferry Panatto and the models to their various destinations: on Tuesday a 'press conference' for fashion writers and a session of photos at Brewers' ad agency; on Wednesday a parade of Panatto's newest line for the lunchtime crowds at the main store. It was all going very smoothly. They were always up when he arrived—Panatto casually and elegantly dressed, usually in blue blazer and grey trousers, eating his scrambled eggs at the breakfast bar, the girls drinking orange juice and checking their make-up.

Thursday. They were in the middle of another photo session. Neil was in awe of the efficient way the girls went about what they had to do. If only he could take a leaf out of their book. Obviously, *they* believed in what they were doing. They were always so cool. They smiled their practised smiles, they were always obliging.

They didn't, however, know how to take Neil. They looked at him curiously from time to time, Barbara in particular, knowing that he was there to serve them, but sensing both that his heart wasn't in what he was doing, and that he lacked confidence. Lack of confidence was something Barbara was able to discern with professional ease.

During the lunch break Barbara approached him as he sat on his own in a director's chair among a pile of photographic gear. She brought a plate of sandwiches with her.

'Hi. Would you like one?'

Neil started and began to get to his feet, suddenly conscious that he should have been the one handing around the sandwiches.

'Oh, sit down! It's alright. You're allowed to have lunch too.'

He took one gratefully.

'Have you been working for this outfit very long, Neil?'

'Only about a month, as a matter of fact.'

'You don't seem to like it very much.'

Here Neil rediscovered something about himself. Greater than his love of the truth was his dislike of being found out. He remained silent. He was being paid to do as he was asked, in this case to be diplomatic, to liaise. He was supposed to feel privileged, being given this assignment.

When he wouldn't respond, Barbara dropped her friendly tone and announced—

'Well if it doesn't make you sick, it should. It's shit work.'

Her final words, before she returned to the business end of the studio, were spoken in a tone of muffled anger—

'What you're doin' is shit work, Neil. Just like what

we're doin' is shit work. We've been with Panatto six months. He's an asshole.'

Neil was stunned. He watched her walk away, and felt his right ear begin to redden.

On the next Monday, the second last day of their visit, Neil arrived at the appointed time but had to knock and knock before Panatto opened the door. It was nine o'clock and they had to be at the main store at nine-thirty for the grand opening of the Panatto Boutique. Panatto was still dressing, his trousers on, but bare-chested. As he hurried Neil in, he asked him in a quiet, panic-stricken way—

'Are we very late?'

Before he could answer, Panatto went on, this time louder—

'They didn't wake me! They didn't wake me today! They didn't wake me. The bitches ... the bitches ...'

Neil watched Panatto pace up and down for a few moments.

'Where are they, the girls?' he asked him.

'They could not last ten days, no. A lousy ten days. They had to let me down.'

Knotting his tie, he nodded in the direction of the door at the end of the suite.

'Please. Would you go, get them up. I can't bear to do it. I can't bear it. I will go crazy at them. Please, you do it. The damn bitches ...'

Neil did as he was told. He knocked but no answer came. He then opened the door and entered, a little scared of what he might find.

There they were. The two women, sitting on the floor, cross-legged, facing each other. They had pulled one of the luggage-racks away from the wall and were using it as a kind of table between them. A game of cards, carefully arranged so as not to fall in between the slats, was spread out on the top of it. They sat quietly, staring at their individual hands. A jug of orange juice and two glasses stood on the floor beside them.

Without looking up from the hand she was holding, Barbara said—

'We know we're late ... Lock the door.'

He did so then returned and waited for her to say something else. He began to feel like a complete idiot. He had no idea what was going on.

'No point in saying anything to us Neil, if that's why you're here,' Barbara spoke again at last.

'No. We have decide. That is all, no more. Over. No more photo. No more Panatto. No more nothing.'

'Ah ...' he opened his mouth, wishing something would come as a consequence.

Barbara put her cards down and stood up.

'Look,' she said, tugging her kimono into place, and pacing slowly around the room, 'you better not think you can talk us out of it or something, if that's why he sent you in ... We've had enough.'

Things were starting to make a little more sense. But Neil still found it hard to believe.

'You're not going to do today's stuff?'

Barbara shook her head violently.

'Or tomorrow's?'

They heard Panatto suddenly bang on the door, once, twice.

'Please!' he shouted. 'Please ...' After a time he tried a different approach. 'You two work for me, you do as I say! Understand?'

The next time he said 'please' it was with a whine in his voice.

It hit Neil—the 'do as I say' part. There was not much that made him hotter and crankier than those little words. Whether they came from his old man, or some big shot fashion designer, made no difference whatsoever. He felt peculiar. Very peculiar. He was overcome by a strange sort of desire to ally himself with these women. Before he could express himself he, as usual, became flushed. But he was going to ignore it. He took his coat off and lowered himself onto his haunches next to Adriana. Barbara joined them on the floor again.

He said softly—

'What will you do?'

Barbara was a little startled. She watched him for a sign that he was trying something. She had expected him to take Panatto's side.

'You're not angry with us?'

'Not a bit.'

Both women were looking at him sceptically now. Why should he take their side? He worked for the department store, after all.

'Why not?' Barbara asked him.

'I don't know ... It's just Brewers. It's unreal, you know, what I've been doing there. I stand behind a counter and sell trousers. Now this. Just bullshit, pure bullshit. Like you said ... I go to these classes but ... It's a con ...' He tried to give a fuller explanation, but the words wouldn't come. Eventually he simply said again what he felt—'It's just bullshit, that's all I can say.'

Barbara raised her glass of orange juice by way of a toast to Neil, a smile so dazzling on her face that he found himself untensing for the first time in days. He fell backwards on the floor and stretched out. He felt like never before, relaxed, relieved.

He raised himself onto his elbow.

'Why did you decide to give it away?'

He saw from the looks on their faces that they hadn't understood what he had said.

'Giving it away, yeah, pulling out now like this.'

Barbara answered—

'Because he's been treatin' us like ... Oh Christ, never mind. You can't think what he's like. What he's been like. We've done England and Canada last couple of months, and he's been lookin' for a lesson. We're givin' him one.'

'Why did you work for him in the first place?'

Barbara got up again and went to the wardrobe. She pulled all her clothes out in a heap and put them on one of the beds. Folding them in readiness for the suitcase, she said—

'I was in Florence, lookin' around, just after I finished

a course in business admin', she turned to Adriana who had also decided it was time to put her things together and was pulling a pair of jeans on, 'and you were workin' in a travel agency there, right?'

'Yes.'

'Panatto was advertising for girls, models, to train as "representatives, if suitable" to take his stuff, his fucking "label", around the world. We would be like "trainees" on this trip.'

Neil nodded, and snorted sarcastically. This was a story he had heard somewhere before. He was going to explain his own status as a trainee when Barbara added—

'It turns out we're suckers. Models my ass. Trainees my ass also. He gave us that "big money, travel, important people" line at the auditions. That was six months ago. He picked us. Here we are. Labour. Cheap labour! All we've seen is hotel rooms, airplanes and catwalks since last September.'

'But you're getting out?'

'We're bookin' planes this mornin', aren't we Adriana?'

Adriana put her arm around Barbara's shoulder. There was a silence. Then Neil made his announcement—

'Well I'm quitting too.'

'Go on!' Barbara thought he was kidding.

'No. That's it. Fuck Brewers!'

'What'll you do?' Barbara asked him.

'I dunno.'

The three of them began to laugh. Softly at first, then louder and louder.

'Hooray for you Neil!' Barbara yelled, partly to cover Panatto's yowling which had recommenced outside the door, but mostly because she felt like it. Adriana too added her own 'bravos'.

'And my name isn't Neil. It's Haralambos.'

Barbara gave him a look of recognition.

'Well, hooray for Haralambos!'

He switched off his calculator. He had finished the figures and checked and rechecked them, but it was still only three o'clock. This happened every Thursday. He never had enough to do to get him through to knock-off time because he never got enough sales figures through from the warehouse to make up a full day's work. He had gone into it, but apparently there was nothing that could be done.

He rearranged the sheets he had been working on a little more neatly and stared down at them for a time. Not that he really cared, but if the clerks down in the warehouse could get their act together, say do their inventory some other day, he wouldn't have to sit here on Thursday afternoons, suffering everybody's eyes.

A little later, at afternoon tea-break, he went to talk to Diane. Her door was generally open at this time to let the tea trolley in. She kept it closed most of the rest of the day because Duncan, the sales manager, didn't like anyone going in there upsetting her—his secretary—unless they had a job to do. Delivering the weekly totals was the only job he had that could legitimately take him in there.

He stood at the door and watched Diane speaking to the tea lady. Josephine, the Maltese one. She was smiling at her as she spoke and that was somehow nice. He would wait until they finished.

He thought how he never had enough time with Diane. On the nights when he went to her place Richard was usually there too and it was hard to talk. Richard was an alright enough bloke, but he was still there between them, and it was hard to get close to her the way he could at work.

The tea lady swung her trolley around and wheeled it out past him. He signalled to Diane with his fingers to check if Duncan was at his desk behind the partition. When she said 'No', he entered.

She was standing beside her desk, sipping her cup of tea.

He said, 'That Josephine's a character, isn't she?'

'She sure is.'

'What was she telling you?' he asked.

'About her mother-in-law. She had a fight with her last night. She told her to get off her property.'

'She's a character alright ... What else did she say?'

Diane put her cup down and made her way around to the other side of her desk. She sat in her chair and looked up at him. With a bit of a smile she said, 'Stop stickybeaking! She was talking to me!'

He replied, 'I know I'm a stickybeak ... She *is* funny though, isn't she ...? Don't you reckon ...?'

She didn't seem to want to reply. He stood and waited with his arms folded. He turned away from her and craned his neck to look through the door and into the outer office, like he was trying to catch something happening there just beyond view.

When he heard her say 'Well …', he shifted around to face her again, but kept his arms folded.

'… she said if she kept having trouble with her, and her hubby didn't do something, she'd pack her own bags and go back to Valetta …'

He said the word 'Valetta' softly. He tried to avoid making it sound like a question, though it must have sounded like one because Diane repeated it.

'Valetta, yes. Do you know what that is?'

'No,' he said quietly.

'It's the capital of Malta.'

He looked away from her once more and said, 'Are you and Richard doing anything tomorrow night?'

'No,' she answered him. 'Do you want to come round?'

'Wouldn't mind.'

Shortly before knock-off time, as he was packing his bag, he heard some laughter coming from the other end of the office. He looked up and saw a group of some of the other admin clerks had formed just inside the door that led to the carpark. They were gathered around someone. That someone soon came out from among them—Barry Banks it was, one of the reps.

Banks, who was holding something behind his back, began waving in his direction. He looked behind him, but there was no one apart from himself down at this end of the office.

'Yes you,' Banks called out to him, 'Do you belong to this?'

Slowly, he brought his hand around from behind his back.

He held up the side-view mirror from somebody's car.

The office was very long, and it was too far away to tell for certain, but from the way all the other clerks were smiling at him, it was a pretty good bet that it was from his car.

'Well Murray, aren't you going to come and have a look?'

They were all standing there, he knew, waiting for him to do something. He took his bag and went towards them.

Banks handed him what was left of the mirror; the glass had been smashed and it had been torn off the mounting. Banks said, 'I found it lying next to the blue Mazda out there—that's yours isn't it?'

'Yes.'

'Looks like one of the trucks swiped it,' Banks said. 'You know how they turn around out there.'

They all kept looking at him—not only Banks, but Forsythe and Cavanagh as well. He wished they would just go away and mind their own business. As they stood and stared and waited, he became angry at them, and finally let it show on his face.

But Forsythe said, 'Don't blame you mate. I'd get the shits too if something like that was done to my car.'

And Cavanagh said, 'Yeah. Better go and find out who did it, Murray.'

He pushed his way past them to get through the door.

Out in the yard, he saw that his was one of only four cars still parked there. Except for himself and those he'd left inside, nearly everyone had left for home. He began to walk across the big expanse of bitumen on which his car looked so small and vulnerable.

He got to it and walked around to the driver's side. Sure enough, it was missing the side-view mirror, and there was a little pile of broken glass on the ground. To top it all off, there was also a scrape mark along the upper part of the door.

The way the truckies used this area to swing their rigs around to get into the warehouse, there was every chance one of them had backed into, or sideswiped, his car. Although there was no evidence of who it might have been, he looked around anyway. He went and looked at the other cars, just in case.

But as he suspected, none of them seemed to have been involved. He realized there was no way he would ever be able to tell who had been responsible. Not without witnesses anyway.

After the replay of the cricket highlights, which he had watched from his bed, it was hard to get to sleep. He tried reading the *TV Week* for a while, but when that didn't help he went and got a beer from the fridge. He turned the television back on and went back to bed where he arranged all the pillows so he could sit up and finish the can of LA. He hardly cared what was on—some kind of American cop movie.

But it was only an hour later, just before one o'clock, when he woke again. The set was still on, running a test pattern; the bedroom was full of a grey half-light. He felt hot and was sweating a little. Pulling the blankets off himself, he swung his legs out and sat on the edge of the bed, trying to clear his head. Then he got up to turn the television off again.

From the bedside table he took up his cigarettes and lighter. When he had lit a cigarette he began to pace slowly up and down in the space between his bed and the TV. He made himself stop eventually, to go instead to the window.

It didn't make sense, worrying about it, but something was telling him he had to make sure. He looked down, saw his car was parked in its usual spot, and looked away again almost immediately. He was stupid for having looked at all, he told himself; it was just being panicky.

He thought of Diane and how he was looking forward to seeing her and, up to a point, Richard, tomorrow night. Were there any other, quicker ways of getting to their flat at Ryde than the one he usually took? As he tried to trace out a different route in his head, something else intruded. He had not had a chance to tell her about the mirror; she had left before it happened.

She pushed the trolley down the aisle to the cashier and got in the queue. It was going to be a long wait by the look of it. On top of it being Friday afternoon, she knew from experience that this was a slow Coles. K-Mart was quicker but the nearest one was at Epping and that was a bit out of the way.

She reached down and pushed aside some of the things she had bought for the weekend to make sure she had in fact picked up a box of corn chips. They were always an easy snack and good with beer. Yes, it was there alright, she hadn't just been imagining she had taken one off the shelf.

They were very handy, these big places. She wondered if they had huge shopping centres like this in Perth too. Then a question she would have to remember to ask Richard—with shops or restaurants, where do they go to buy their stuff? The stuff they sell? It seemed a pretty obvious question, but then she had never had any reason to ask it up till now.

Her turn at the register and the girl began to lift the things out of her trolley. She punched up the price of each item, then moved everything further along the counter to another girl who began packing it all into paper bags.

Waiting for her to finish she thought of earlier this afternoon, when Murray had come in for his usual tea-break visit. He had with him something wrapped in a piece of paper, like a present. He had asked her to guess what it was. She told him she had no idea, he opened it, and there was the mirror from a car. It was boring, the way he had gone on and on about it; how it had happened yesterday afternoon; how one of the truckies was probably responsible.

Funny the way he looked at her when she told him that didn't surprise her—that was the way they were, the drivers who worked for this company. He had been looking at her the way you do when you're listening really hard, when you're trying to hear above the noise from something.

'Richard and I agreed about that—not having too much furniture—when we first came here.'

He shifted on Diane's lounge and looked at the fabric, and said, 'I reckon you've got enough.'

She said, 'The way we've been moving around the last few years, it's easier that way—you can travel light. And a small flat like this—it's easier to keep clean ...'

There was silence for a time as *Sale of the Century* took their attention—one of the challengers picked up fifteen points in a row on the champion.

In the commercial break, he leaned across to the arm of the lounge and took some corn chips from the bowl.

Richard said, 'That's right, have some more. Diane bought a big box, didn't you love.'

'I sure did,' Diane said.

'You're very quiet tonight Murray,' Richard said, as he himself came over from his armchair to take some chips. When he returned to his seat he asked, 'How are they treating you at work?'

'Alright. Had some trouble with the car though ...'

'Diane said about that. Couldn't find who did it, ay? Ah well, you see, that's what it's like these days. Nobody takes responsibility for anything any more ... It's like where I am. In the Defence Department nobody gives a stuff either. You'd think in the *Defence Department* ... You should see the waste. I tell 'em—ah Christ, I'm always telling 'em—but does anybody listen ...? No way mate, no bloody way ...'

Diane turned in her chair to face Richard. 'It's the same here as when you were in Melbourne, isn't it darling?'

'Too right it is Di ... Bureaucracy is the same wherever you go.'

Sale of the Century came back on. After the next lot of questions the lady who was last night's champion had got a good lead back. It was boring when this happened, she thought. As her interest began to wane, she looked over at her husband and tried to remember some of the things he had said earlier. The way he included people, like poor Murray, was something she respected about Richard.

He had a lot of other good points, like being trust-worthy and reliable. You had to be reliable if you had a business, she assumed, or no one would come to you. She tried to imagine what living in Perth would be like. That clipping from her mother who had herself moved to WA recently—Service Station and Roadhouse in prime position ... she had forgotten to ask him if he'd made any enquiries in the last few days. He would be happy in his own business, she knew he would.

Richard came in from the bathroom with a towel around him. From the bed she saw that he was dripping water.

'Look out, you're dripping water on the carpet,' she said.

He rubbed himself some more with the towel and moved over to the dressing table to look at himself in the mirror.

'Stuff the carpet ...'

'But you know how the landlord's always ...'

He picked up one of her brushes and began to do his hair. He said, 'Not for much longer, he won't ...' and continued to look in the mirror.

She didn't take in his meaning for a moment. Then she thought she did, but she had to ask him, 'Are you being serious?'

'Dead serious,' he said. 'I intend to buy that business.'

He turned around at last, but his face wasn't changing. She still found it hard to believe.

'We're really going to buy that place?'

'I sure am.'

He came to the bed and she threw the sheet down so he could get in. When he was beside her, he rolled over to her side and propped himself on an elbow.

She said, 'I'm scared now. I hope it's the right thing.'

He put a hand on one of her breasts and began to knead it.

'I was always meant to work for myself,' he said. 'Just a waste of time it was, being in the public service. A total waste of time.'

It felt a little uncomfortable, what he was doing. But with all the things that were crowding into her mind, she didn't notice after a while.

'Gee I hope it works out Richard ... Poor old Murray will be disappointed when I tell him we're going.'

He replied, 'Hard to get rid of him tonight, wasn't it?' He moved his hand away and put it on her knee. And now he smiled at her. She saw, however, that it was only a pretend smile.

He said, 'I was right, wasn't I? If I'd let you make a lot of friends here, it would've been a lot harder for us to pack up and go now, wouldn't it?'

He ran his hand down over her knee and between her legs. But when he tried to move them apart, even though he was going slowly and gently, he found resistance.

It was a good afternoon, Monday, a bit busier than the others because all the orders from country food markets had been filled and there were plenty of figures to work with. This Monday was extra busy because he had been asked to do a breakdown of tinned fruit sales in the western region. Duncan had told him after lunch that he had spotted a downhill trend in the figures over the last few months. He wanted a comparison to last year so he could get onto the reps about it.

He had just about wrapped up this job and was re-checking his additions on the calculator, when he saw Banks come in and begin making his way around the other desks to where he was sitting.

Once he was by his side, he bent over and said softly, 'Hey Murray, got some news for you. Talking to one of the blokes in the loading dock, and guess what ...'

'What?'

'He knows who did it ... who rammed your car last week.'

Banks didn't straighten up, but put his hands on his knees and stayed there like he was waiting for something.

'Well?' he began again. 'Do you want to know or don't you?'

'Yes,' he said, 'I want to know.'

'It was one of the drivers,' Banks said. 'By the name of Woodcock ... You can do something about it now, can't you?'

'Yes, suppose I can now. Yes ...'

Banks nodded a couple of times and finally stood up straight again. Taking some steps away from his desk, he said, 'So I'll leave you to it, ay? See you later. And make sure you don't let them get away with anything ...'

He watched Banks walk to the far end of the office. After he was gone, he gathered up the sheets he had been working on and pushed his chair away from the desk. Should Duncan be around when he entered his office, the sheets would be a good excuse.

Diane was typing when he entered.

She stopped and smiled at him. 'Hello Murray,' she said. 'I thought afternoon tea was over ...?'

'I just found out something.'

'Oh yes ...?'

'I know who hit my car ... Remember? The broken mirror?'

She switched off the typewriter.

'You're not *still* going on about that, are you? It's not really worth that much trouble, is it?'

What she had said made him feel awkward. It was like she wanted to stop him from saying anything else. But he decided he was still allowed to have his say. He said, 'But it *is* a new car you know, and ...'

'Speaking of new things, you've reminded me. I've got something to tell *you* ... Richard and I are moving to Perth. We're going to buy a business there. Our own business ... What do you think about that ...?'

Again she had thrown him. But what he had just heard was worse, far worse. He turned away from her and went to the partition, pretending to be interested as to whether Duncan was behind it. Duncan wasn't in, but he stayed there facing the partition.

He said, 'That'll be nice ... The only thing those bastards deserve is a bullet between the eyes. Got half a mind to go and buy a gun ... That's what they deserve ...'

He wheeled around and paced his way to the door, holding up the sheets.

'Talk to you later. Better go and finish these.'

He returned to his desk and sat down. He put his head in his hands and started to push his fingers through his hair. Now his eyes began to feel watery ...

Just when he believed he was making some progress with her ... Only a proper bitch could have done this to him. Who would have thought she could be such a bitch? Such a bitch ... Who would have thought ...

Some time later he had settled down enough to be able to open the sheets and put them in front of him, to at least look like he was doing something. He felt better now because at least one possible answer had presented itself. But he had yet to work out the total cost—the number of tanks of petrol it would take to get to Perth, times the price of a tank. He switched on his calculator.

I TOLD MAMA NOT TO COME

Whether he was born with it, or whether it started when he was a kid, I'm not sure. If it started when he was a kid I'd like to know exactly when, how, who was to blame.

This morning I've been trying to remember the last time I ever saw him. In fact, I've been trying to recall all the people who have gone out of my life. I thought I'd start with the ones who had something wrong with them and so Dionysios, Denny, has come back to life in my head this morning. Why the sick ones? Because I've got a few questions. You can't help it when you've been sick yourself.

My mother reminded me of Denny when she was in here visiting me yesterday. She saw Denny's mother in the street from a distance. She thought it was Denny's mother. She hadn't seen her for years, hadn't spoken to her since they had an argument when we were kids. She's the one who really got me going, thinking about Denny. She always makes things worse by holding things back, not telling me the whole story when I want to know more. I can't help thinking about it then.

If I was about ten, which seems right, it would have been 1961. I must have been about ten the last time we visited the family Zagaris—Costas, Theocline, and son Dionysios. That last visit itself I can't remember. But there's not much to do in here and I've been putting it back together pretty good. I know the story, I know what it must have been like, if it was like any of the others.

They ran a food shop, same as we did. Theirs was in Sans Souci, and ours was in Newtown. My parents came from the island of Mytilene, like his, that's how they knew each other. The Zagarises had their home away from the shop—in Ramsgate or maybe Kogarah—so they must have been doing better than my parents. Denny was an only child, like myself. But if I was ten in 1961 he must have been pushing twenty, for sure.

We used to catch the tram out along Rocky Point Road, mama and I, on the Sundays we went visiting. My father never came with us because he had to keep the shop open. He always had to keep the shop open. His excuse was that we needed the money that came in on Sundays when the 'big shops' were closed. But Denny's father was always home on Sundays. He even went to church, which my old man never did.

Of the tram trip out I can't recall too much. One thing. There were trees, palm trees I think, along a kind of narrow island between the tracks.

They lived in a brick place, really something to me who lived in the weatherboard rooms behind our shop. A red brick house, a palace with a lawn out the front and a garage at the side. We must have been the poor folks. That's probably the main reason my father didn't want to come. He hated anybody who was making money.

I had nothing like the amount of junk Denny had

been given. He had everything, but I see now that this was part of his problem. Dionysios had an electric train set, a Meccano set, and an incredible number of *National Geographics* among other things. He spent his life with toys, but, as I say, he would have been nearly twenty. He was mentally retarded. The ten years between us made no difference. We were the same age.

What we did together that afternoon wouldn't have been very exciting, or so different to what we usually did, which was to play. We would have cleared a space in the middle of his room, and got one of the toys out. If it was the trainset (he had a Hornby, the best), he would have pulled it out from under his bed, and silently pieced the track together, and just as silently made the thing run.

He hardly ever let me work the switches. The magazines were another thing. Those, which he kept in cardboard boxes I think, he would let me flick through myself, unless there was a new one. A new one he would have to show me himself. He would stop at a picture that amused him and he would smile very quietly and point it out. I can't remember how I acted, probably just nodded so he wouldn't get upset. Sometimes for some reason or other he would get tears in his eyes and I would have to go and get his mother.

We had to be watched anyway. Every so often one or other of the mothers would open the door to see if everything was alright. If the sweets had been produced in the living room, sometimes a few would be brought in to us. Mrs Zagaris, like my mother, always went in for serving coffee and sweets to visitors. A little cup of black syrupy stuff would be brought in to the living room, along with a glass of water, and a plate of *kourabies*, or preserved fruits with a little spoon. All on a showy, chrome tray. Whatever was left, we had to finish.

What was the argument about? What could they, who had so much in common, have argued about? When she was here yesterday ... (this morning?) ... she didn't want to talk about it when I asked her. But after a while she had to tell me or I would've got upset, wouldn't I? She thinks she has to humour me because I am in here. What it was about, she said after I kept at her, was that over the years she had become more and more annoyed at the way Mrs Zagaris was bringing up her son. Instead of encouraging him to grow up, she kept treating him like a little boy. He had a problem, yes, but she was making things worse, spoiling him, always buying him toys, always sheltering him, no wonder he turned out the way he did.

I don't know if what she told me was the truth or not. It's too hard to believe. That my mother would castigate anyone for mollycoddling their kid. What a laugh. My old lady has won ribbons for it herself. That's one of the reasons I turned out the way I did, no risk.

The number of people my parents have told about my own thing you could count on your fingers. And I'm redeemable! Just a bit of a nervous collapse, nothing serious, but enough to put me in here for a while, and enough to put her on her best behaviour. The old man's just as bad though. When he comes at all, he gets all jolly, like I've got a broken leg or something, or like nothing's happened and I'm here just for something to do.

No, I don't believe this story of my mother falling out with Denny's mother about bringing up children. What could they have argued about? What was so different about the way she brought me up? I was kept indoors. I was bought books to keep me distracted or occupied so that I wouldn't bother anybody. I wasn't allowed to join anything, like the cubs, or sports. Couldn't go to the beach because I would drown. Couldn't go to the school dances because the girls there were no good. Little Golden Books and a World Encyclopedia from Woolworths. She even used to bring my lunch to school and feed me in a corner of the playground! With all the other kids watching and laughing.

When I get out I'm going to try and find him, see how he is now, what he is up to. You never know, he might be OK. I reckon that where we all went wrong was in losing contact with each other. We should have stuck together. People like Denny, funnily enough, could help me a lot today. Even if I am thirty, it's not too late.

Or what about Peter? Peter from up the road whose old man worked in the drum factory. They shunned him because he did no good at school and he nearly went crazy too. He kept running away and the police had to keep bringing him back. But he turned out alright in the end. He joined an airline and flew away forever. Into the skies, the beautiful, huge skies. I'd like to see him again too if I could find him.

He finally got away. He left his mother and father and

started his own life. He had to stop being the good, obedient, respectful son. I tried to stop being those things too, but tried staying at home at the same time. It didn't work, and all I got was fights. So many, many fights. It's a wonder I never killed one of them. For a while I thought I *had* killed someone. For about a year I thought I had killed someone. I wasn't sure who, but I had this tremendous feeling of guilt. It's gone now, thank Christ.

They should be bringing lunch around soon. I asked for fish fillets. What a laugh, they give you one bit and it always has bones. One thing I could never get at mama about was the food she cooked, which was always fantastic ...

She usually brings me something extra when she comes around, which I hope she doesn't do today. I'm having a good day, and I've got quite a lot to think about and work out ...

No, I can't remember any harsh words or red faces that afternoon. There must be some other reason why we stopped going to Denny's which she hasn't told me about. Maybe she really had the argument with *Mr* Zagaris. But about what? ... Maybe some sex thing. Maybe they were having it off ...

Ha! My mother would never do that sort of thing, even if she wasn't religious. She just wouldn't do it to me.

I told mama not to come, but I hope she does come today. I'm starting to miss her again. And I've still got some questions to ask her. With her help I'll be able to get out of here soon, no worries. I'm feeling better. I hope she does come.

THE JIGSAW PUZZLE

She hoped that dopey son of hers hadn't had a crash or something. He was supposed to have Becky back from the airport ages ago—it was now three o'clock. The sandwiches had gone already, and she'd been obliged to heat up the prawn mornay and serve it long before she wanted to. But with the way sister Em and her nieces and nephews had attacked it—not to mention her own bunch—it too was in danger of disappearing before her other sister arrived. Talk about being good on the tooth.

She went to Em.

'How long would you say it takes Em? From the airport.'

'You should allow for customs too, you know.'

'I'm allowing an hour for that.'

'Let's see ... The plane's supposed to arrive at twelve, and you're allowing an hour for the airport business ... I'd say half an hour for the drive here ... so that makes it one-thirty. They should have been here at one-thirty, Frances.'

'That's what *I* would have said ... Do you think we should ring or something?'

'Ring? Where?'

She was stumped—and not for the first time this

afternoon. Em was a great one for tripping you up; and she was also a great one for remaining cool and calm. That was alright for her. It wasn't her silly eighteen-year-old son who had got his licence a few months back and who was the biggest tearaway in Cabramatta.

'Stop worrying,' Em said. 'Give me your glass and let me get you another drink.'

Em took Frances's tumbler and went to the bar in the corner of the living room.

Frances looked around and thought everyone seemed happy enough. None of the boys had got pissy as yet—which was a bonus. Except for this hitch with Becky's arrival, she was pretty content with the way things had got going. She liked having people around, but it was hard to get them together like this. It usually only happened when you had something special.

Seeing Em take a can of VB from the bar fridge, she waved to her. But Em's husband Phil got in the way, so she had to duck across to her quickly.

'Wait on Em. Wait. Not VB for me. I'll have some of that light stuff, if there's any left.'

Em put the offending can back and found one of the right sort. She pulled the ring and filled the glass.

'There you are, my girl.'

'Ta.'

Frances took a sip and went around the end of the bar counter and joined her sister.

'Yes, that's right,' said Em, 'come and enjoy the view. You get a good view from around here ...'

Em ran her hand along the top of the bar, and then along one edge.

'He's done a good job hasn't he? Putting vinyl on the sides and all that.'

'Oh yes. He's good with his hands alright.'

'It was his idea, I suppose, was it?'

'Certainly was Em.'

They looked at each other—they knew each other's lot very well indeed—and began to laugh.

'Never mind,' Em jollied her. 'You've got to let them get away with *something*. Or you never get any peace.'

'Too true, too true. But a bar *is* handy for entertaining like this, I think ... Speaking of entertaining, I'd better have another look at the snack situation.'

Because she had moved the coffee table out of the way to make more room, the savoury and sandwich plates and the bowl with the mornay were arranged on the top of the pianola and on the shelves of the room divider. This had turned into a messy arrangement, however. The kids had made sure they scattered plenty of chips and nuts around the place, and so she bent down to the carpet now to pick up as many whole pieces as she could find. She was going to take these scraps out to the kitchen, but finished up dropping them into an ashtray instead.

Not only was the mess starting to get to her, so was the noise. She thought she would give herself a break and go out to the laundry where they were keeping the main supply of soft drinks. There, she dug through the ice in the tub to find a bottle of lemonade and one of cola. She found herself playing with the ice, smoothing it back over the remaining bottles.

It had probably been a mistake sending Brad out to the airport. It was her husband's idea—'how would *you* like a great crowd waitin' for you after you'd been on a plane so long?' It would give her time to get her bearings, he had also said. But she wasn't sure about that. Surely she would want somebody at the airport to greet her. But there you are, the boys had talked her out of it, and they had all stayed put to get everything ready and welcome her to the place where she would be living for the next little while.

She had spent a lot of time thinking about how well Becky would be able to get used to things; it wasn't like old England here. Not any more anyway. Coming out to Australia had changed her, as it had changed Em. But it wasn't so much that they had changed as they had got used to different things. How would Becky, the last of the Pearson girls, the one who had stayed on in Leeds where they'd been born, how would she cope with it all?

She came back up from the yard with the bottles—only to find her husband now wrestling with young Craig in the middle of the living room. A space had been cleared and Phil was standing there cheering them on. Les had his arm around the youngest's head and was grinning and making some awful animal noise at the same time.

'Let him go Les. You'll hurt him.'

'I'm not hurtin' him,' he said. He pulled him down to the floor where they began to roll around. Their laughing gave way to shouts as they banged their heads on the floor and then on the side of the lounge.

Frances raised her voice—'See what I mean?'—and tried to get hold of the boy. But Craig saw her coming and called out—

'We're only muckin' around Mum, don't worry.'

'Just stop it and get up will you!'

Les let go of him and slowly got up on his knees. He was out of breath and his puffing made it harder to tuck his shirt tails back into his trousers. Craig meanwhile was already up and looking for a new distraction.

'Righto you,' his father began in a fond sort of way, 'Take those off your mother, go on.'

His mother gave him the bottles and he took them to the bar. Les got to his feet and the area they had used as an arena soon filled with people again. He came up to Frances.

'What were you gettin' so upset about? I was just *playin'* with him … Anyway, I know what's really buggin' you.'

'Well you tell me then. What's happened to them?'

'Alright, alright, I'll ring the airport if it'll stop the carry on.

'I wish you would, instead of making a nuisance of yourself in here.'

Brad was a bit worried about the time all this was taking. He knew he was expected to be back before this, but there was nothing he could have done about the flight being delayed, or the time it took for his aunt's bags to turn up on that carousel thing. And to hold things up even more, she had wanted him to drive slowly so she would have a chance to look at the scenery along the way to home. There was no scenery as far as he could see, but he couldn't have said that—he was supposed to be on his best behaviour.

His mother had told him to take it easy with Aunt Becky because she would probably be tired from the flight. But from where he was standing—at the doorway of a newsagency in Cabramatta—his aunt definitely did not look tired.

Aunt Becky was inside, looking for gifts for the kids. As she had meant to pick up something in Singapore for them, but had forgotten, she had asked Brad to stop at some shops so she could have a look for something. He had pulled up at this little row of shops in Fitzgerald Street, which was apparently quite close to their destination, but leaving aside the food shops, this newsagency seemed to be the only possibility.

Surprised at how few shops there were along the route, she had said as much to Brad. He had told her of a big new shopping centre, a 'mall' he had called it, but according to him it was too far to go and they wouldn't have enough time before it shut. So she had been reduced to this place. Luckily, there was a selection of toys and games to choose from in here.

The only difficulty was getting someone to serve her. The girl at the cash register had directed her to the assistant at the back of the shop—but that one was busy serving. Waiting her turn, she wandered along the length of the magazine rack. Some of the magazines were familiar from home—*Woman*, *Titbits*, *The Guardian Weekly*. She took up a copy of *Woman* and looked at the cover—two months out of date it was—but anyhow it was nice to know such familiar things as this were available here.

She looked again at the girl in the depths of the shop. Still busy with someone. She went down to see what was causing the delay. The assistant and her customer were in front of the greeting card stand; there seemed to be some kind of argument going on. Moving closer, she understood what the trouble was.

'You said you wanted birthday cards,' the assistant was saying to an Asian girl of some kind, 'well, these are birthday cards.'

But the Asian girl wouldn't say anything, just kept staring down at the cards she was holding.

'Who are they for? Are they for a brother or sister or father or what?'

Becky felt some sympathy for the girl—she had always found it hard herself trying to get through to someone who didn't speak English. She could tell the assistant was getting impatient, the way she was looking over the head of the girl and in her direction. When their eyes met, Becky gave her a little smile back and mouthed the words 'when you are ready'. The assistant nodded to her. Very friendly too, that nod was, she couldn't help but think.

As this was taking so long, it would be best if she first had a look over the toys herself.

She went around the magazine rack to the wall opposite her where a large pink bear of some kind had caught her eye. Yes, this was the part. A small selection, but with a bit of variety, and that was a relief—she did want to get the lad something. There were toy cars and plastic models and games in boxes. She remembered Ludo and Snakes and Ladders, but there weren't any of those—most of the boxes had names like Dungeons and Dragons. As well, there were quite a few jigsaw puzzles. Nice ones, some of them.

She had taken one off the shelf and was inspecting it more closely when the assistant finally came to her side.

'Sorry to keep you waiting,' she said.

'Never mind love. It takes time when they don't speak the language, I know ...'

She read the cover—'200 Pieces' it said, and 'Endless Fun for All Ages'. The picture was of a Beefeater. She saw the price too, but as dollars weren't as much as pounds, she didn't worry too much that it seemed so high.

'Think I'll take this one.'

The girl peered down at it, yet said nothing. Becky regarded her for a second or two. Not very with it, she concluded. Shopgirls are the same wherever you go.

'Handsome isn't he? Do you think a ten-year-old will like it?'

'Suppose. What kind of uniform is that anyway?'

'What kind of uniform? Oh dear, you ought to know

that. It's a Yeoman of the Guard, isn't it? A Beefeater!'

'Oh,' she replied, and leaned forward to find a few more to show her.

'Don't bother. Give me another two of this sort, please.'

She took them to the counter at the front and waved to Brad leaning against the window to come and have a look.

'What do you say, Brad? Will our Craig like it for instance?'

He shrugged his shoulders and said—'Oh yeah ... Probably.' The truth about his brother was that he was into Pac-Man and BMX bikes and that was *it*. Running late, he couldn't afford any more delays like having Aunt Becky start looking all over again. As it was, sorting out his aunt's money for her was going to cause another hold-up.

They were out in the street, and heading back to the car, when Becky put a hand on his arm. She wanted him to stop outside one particular shop.

'Why is it all spread out everywhere like that?'

She pointed to a few sacks of nuts and some large tins of something or other which were arranged around the entrance to a food shop. They were taking up part of the footpath.

'Are they allowed to do that? It's not allowed back home ...'

She stood back and tried to read the name on the window.

'Can't make that out, can you Brad?'

'It's Lebo, I think.'

Tilting her upper body to see inside, her hand went to the plumpness of her side. Something had hurt there, and Brad noticed her grimace. And then, as if she were cross with herself, she started to shake her head.

'Come on nephew. That's what I get for dawdling.'

They heard the car horn and the suspense was over. Frances went for the door but was beaten by Craig who had it open and was outside in a flash. After that, everyone seemed to spill out into the front yard all at once. What with Em and Phil and Tracy and Steven, and her own Les and Craig and old Mrs Bardwell from next door, all crowding around, Frances couldn't get to her for a while. In the moment before she was able to get close enough to give her a hug and a kiss, she ordered Brad and Craig to carry the bags inside.

Then, the longed-for contact. And the crying.

'Welcome Becky. Welcome ... It's so good ...'

Becky tried to say something, but found herself being almost carried in the direction of the house. She lost contact with Fran who was suddenly behind her rather than in her arms.

She was very happy to get inside out of the strong sun though. Feeling it for the first time as she walked out of the airport building and across that furnace of a parking lot, she had been conscious of it ever since.

'Phew!' she called out. 'Let me sit down, I just have to sit down. I haven't got used to your heat yet I'm afraid!'

As if by instinct, she went for the lounge. She handed

the coat she was carrying to one of the men—she didn't know who it was for the time being—but hung on to her parcel. She lowered herself carefully and put the gifts to one side, at the same time brushing away some hair which had strayed onto her forehead.

A kind of path opened up for Frances and Em to get close to her. The men—Les and Phil and Les's brother Roger who had not bothered coming outside earlier— all stood back. Les, seeing that Craig was getting a bit hysterical from the excitement, pointed a threatening finger at him—this was a time for the girls, and they were entitled to a bit of quiet.

Frances was the first to sit down next to her—Em was about to do likewise but instead asked her if she wanted something to drink.

'Yes please, something cool.' This sister left and she faced the other. 'I was alright on the aeroplane you know. It never worried me at all.'

'Well I've fixed up a room for you and you can lie down and have a rest if you're feeling too tired.'

'No, no, *I'll* be alright.'

Em returned with a glass of lime cordial. She handed it to her carefully and sat down on the opposite side to Frances. She watched her take a sip and exclaimed 'God! You're just like the photos, Becky, you haven't changed one bit!' Fran followed with 'You are, you've never changed.'

'Don't flatter me girls,' she replied. 'I'm pushing sixty, as you well know.'

This touched something in all of them and they began to cry. First Frances, then Em, and in the end, Becky as well. Fran and Em embraced her from each side.

From the looks on their faces, Brad and Craig obviously thought this was pretty funny. Craig even put on a little mocking act, pretending to cry behind the hand he held in front of his face. Their father sidled up to them quietly.

'Behave yourselves, you two. And I want a word with you,' he poked Brad in the stomach, 'about how long it took you to get here.'

'Me? It was *her* who was holding me up.'

He had spoken in a loud whisper which annoyed his father even more.

'Don't you give cheek—I know you a bit better than that, sonny Jim.'

Brad raised his voice good and proper this time—'Aw don't give me the shits!'—and stamped away to another part of the room. Frances, having heard his carry-on, followed him with her eyes as he went to sulk in a corner—he had folded his arms and was shaking his head. When he glanced her way, she put her finger to her lips. This, however, only worked to make him angrier, and the next anyone knew he was out the door. His father was about to go after him, but within seconds he heard the car door slam, the engine rev up, and his smart arse of a son race away doing wheelies.

Although Em had been talking to her all the way through this, Becky was not unaware of what had been happening. She touched Fran to get her attention.

'Anything wrong?'

'Oh just the eldest. He's getting a bit stroppy these days—they all do at his age.'

'Boys are a *trouble*, aren't they?' she replied, smiling a rueful smile, partly to herself, partly for her sister's benefit. She put a hand on each of their knees. 'No, you two, can't say I envy you with all these *children* of yours!' She followed with a silly, playful sort of laugh and then asked—'Does he have a job, young Brad? I meant to ask him before.'

'Well ...' Frances began, but was cut off before she could get any further.

'Never mind. He'll have to work one day ... It's better for them over here, I've heard. They're *all* on the dole over there, you know. *All* of them, the young lads. It's disgraceful really. They won't work. They won't do anything for themselves ...'

Les, who since the altercation had been content just to gaze down at his sister-in-law and drink his beer, now took a new interest in her. He moved across the room a couple of steps, the better to be able to address her more directly.

'No, you're right there. They *definitely won't*. That Prime Minister of yours has got the right idea. She's a tough one that one, they reckon.'

When Les moved even closer again, Frances stood up. He had got Becky's attention, and it looked like he was getting ready to give her his two bob's worth. It was surprising, however, that Becky was all ears. They were great mates already; in a way, that annoyed her, although she wasn't quite sure why that was.

She interrupted them.

'Give me your coat from behind you there, Becky. I can see it's making you hot.'

'Hm?' Becky's head went in all directions until she realized it was Fran, standing above her, who had spoken. 'Oh. Alright …' She handed it up. 'But I want to keep this …' she tapped the parcel, 'for the time being.'

Fran went to the spare bedroom, set up for Becky's stay, and threw the coat on the bed. She sat down beside it and took part of the material between her fingers to feel it. It was wool and so heavy. And old-fashioned. You didn't need a coat like that in Sydney, ever. It was a real English winter coat and it got her thinking.

She hadn't actually given much thought to what Becky was like—only to whether she would be able to get used to things and whether she would be able to fit in. Most of her energy had gone into talking Les around to letting her stay in the first place, to give her time to work out if she wanted to stay for good—there wasn't much family left for her in England any more. But after what she had just seen in the living room, it didn't look like there was going to be any problem between them.

Not between *them* … She was feeling a bit disappointed. Something was wrong. Her sister seemed sort of wrapped up in herself … And the way she was straight off talking about Brad not having a job …

Every now and then she heard that funny laugh of Becky's coming through the door. She tried not to notice, but it was a stupid sort of a laugh. Like a little girl's. She was the eldest, but there was something really *young* about her. *Silly* young. That's what happened, she surmised, when you didn't have kids of your own.

Whatever it was they'd been talking about, when she came back out, it was finished. Les had retreated to a corner with his brother. Becky was sitting all by herself. She was cross with them for having left her like that, and went to her side straight away.

'They're naughty, aren't they, leaving you on your own like this.'

'Not at all. Emma's going to show me some photos,' she said. 'She's gone to get the photos.'

A silence followed, an awkwardness which was relieved only when Becky started to fan herself.

'Oh dear, this heat must be really getting to you—I didn't think to write about how hot it can get ... Do you want another drink? Or I can turn the air-conditioner on.'

'Air-conditioner?'

'Yes. Oh, I forgot. They probably don't have ...'

'Frances, we *do* have those in England. I haven't come from Mars or something—no, it's better for me to get used to it. It's not that bad in here ...'

Em reappeared. She was carrying a pile of albums retrieved from the top of the wardrobe in her sister's bedroom.

'Gee. You mustn't have looked at 'em for a while, sis. They're as dusty as anything.'

'Em, Becky's probably just going to get bored with all these.'

'No I won't Frances. What makes you say that?'

The way she said that—it put her back in the days of some of these photos better than the photos themselves did. Back to when her eldest sister was always there to tick her off.

Em opened one of the books and put it on Becky's lap. She started out with the ones they had brought over with them when they had emigrated, ones that were familiar to them all. The one outside the house with dear dead Mum, and Dad in his uniform. The one where they'd gone down to London to meet him when he was being discharged, and they were all going to stay with rich Aunt Lorna for a holiday.

Then the photos from here, the Australian ones. These interested her more, especially the photos of Brad and Craig when they were babies. She looked and looked at those.

'Look at this one,' she lowered her voice, 'this one of Brad ... you can tell from his face, he's a cheeky one. He's going to be a cheeky one.' She asked Em—'Don't you think? Doesn't he look the young rebel already?'

Frances allowed herself a little annoyance.

'Come on, Beck. You can't tell anything from a *photo*. It's just a photo.'

'No, no. I think you can see things in photos, I really do.'

Fran felt like shutting up for a while. The idea that her sister had already started putting her in her place was depressing. Em kept turning the pages, showing this and explaining that, but she was happier keeping out of it. It was hard to stay interested in all these pictures she'd seen a thousand times before—even if some of them were new to Becky.

Only when Em leaned across to ask her about one in particular did she feel obliged to make an effort again.

'What year was this picnic, Fran?'

She pointed out a photo where the kids, hers and Fran's, were in a park somewhere and wearing fancy dress.

'That was the Leagues Club Picnic, wasn't it—'79 or '80 I think—'80, yes '80.'

Becky looked at this one closely too.

'Ooh, aren't some of the costumes way out ... What are they wearing? I can see Craig here, yes, that's him. What is it he's wearing? Funny isn't it?'

Em supplied the answers.

'He's dressed up as a Chinaman. See?' She pointed out the details with her little finger. 'He's got that hat they have. And a pigtail, we made a pigtail for him ... We even put sticky tape on his eyes, you know, to make them go all slanty.'

'Oh my goodness!' Becky lifted her chin and began to laugh. It turned into a long and noisy cackle. Frances grinned at the sound, but then she couldn't help it, she laughed too, it was so infectious.

It was a great relief. When they had got hold of themselves again, she felt better, more relaxed. Whatever, it was good to be able to laugh with old Becky again. Maybe things would work out alright after all.

As for Becky, she put on a conspiratorial tone and asked her—'Where is he anyway? Where is the boy? I've got something for him. I may as well start handing them out, mayn't I?'

'You didn't have to bother. Don't think he was expecting to get anything.'

'What kind of an aunt would I be if I didn't bring presents—I didn't get anything for Brad, mind. Only the young ones—Craig—and your two Em ... But where is the little Chinaman?'

Fran called out—'Craig? ... Where are you?'

He appeared from behind the room divider; he had been lying on the floor there, playing with his mini-computer game.

'Oh *there* you are. Come here for a sec, will you?'

He approached dutifully.

'Now Craig, Aunt Becky's got something she wants to give you.'

'Yes, that's right lad. Come on. Come closer. But before I give it to you, I want to ask you ... Is this really you in this picture? Here, look ...' she showed him the album photo. 'Is that you dressed up like that?'

Craig looked down. He didn't care much about pictures of himself; you always had to be getting dressed up for them.

'Yeah,' he nodded, 'that's me.'

'You were a Chinaman, were you?'

'Yeah.'

'Oh dearie me ...' For a moment it was a possibility

that she would start laughing again, but she got a grip on herself in time.

Because he had an idea he was supposed to say something more, Craig went on—

'There's a lot of Chinese kids in our class this year.'

'Vietnamese,' his mother corrected him.

'Yeah, I mean Vietnamese.'

Becky had a rather more serious aside for his mother. 'I was meaning to ask you ... down at the shops where Brad took me, I saw quite a few Oriental people. Are there a lot of them here too then?'

'Yes,' Em put in. ''Fraid so. They're coming out all the time.'

Becky was about to say something further when Craig asked—'Can I go now Mum?' But Becky took his hand in one of hers, and with her free hand tore open the parcel which was perched on the back of the lounge behind her. It was difficult, but she was determined to do it this way, that is, hanging on to the boy at the same time. With Em's help she eventually freed one of the puzzles and brought it round in front of her.

'This is for you my boy ... Go on, you can have a look.'

He took it from her and looked at it sheepishly. 'Well, what do you say?'

'Thanks.'

'No, I mean what do you think of it?'

As this was something he'd never seen before, he wasn't sure what to say. His mother prompted him—'Oh look, it's a jigsaw puzzle. You've never had one of those have you?'

'No, I've never had one of these.'

Becky was a bit taken aback.

'Oh my goodness. Oh dear. Anyhow, I'll show you how to do it later, you'll like it I'm sure ... Look at the picture. What about that, ay? It's a handsome picture, really and truly. You know what *he* is, don't you?'

Craig was silent again.

'He's a Beefeater. You know them, don't you? Don't you ...?'

Craig shook his head shyly.

Becky patted him on the hand.

'Don't worry. Don't worry.' She turned to Fran, 'I can see I'll have plenty to talk to this young chappie about.' And then back to Craig—'There's lots of things Auntie can tell you, Craig. Beefeaters is only the start.'

THE CHEERFULNESS OF THE BUSH

She had got away, and crossed the river, and was on her way to Robertson. But not without a hassle. The radiator of her little Renault was overheating, which meant having to drive very slowly. To make things worse, the push-button radio had become stuck on her father's station. Unable to get the ABC she had, for the last twenty minutes, resigned herself to listening to her father give the Produce Report.

By the end of his session, however, she was no longer listening; his voice had become just a noisy background for her thoughts. She had turned to thinking about *The Snow Leopard*, a book she had read recently. It was not the sort of book she normally read, but it had pleased her; going to a part of the Co-Op bookshop she had never given much notice before, and picking it up on a whim, and reading right through it.

She reached down into the space between her seat and the brake to make sure it was still there. She had liked the title, and the way it began—'In late September of 1973, I set out with GS on a journey to the Crystal Mountain, walking west under Annapurna and north along the Kali Gandaki River ...'

There were people in the world who had walked through northwest Nepal in search of a leopard seen only twice in twenty-five years. People who were acquainted with the Buddhist Monasteries of Inner Dolpo. By comparison, what was she acquainted with? Grenville and Robertson, those were the places she knew best. And the muddy stream between them.

She wished she might have been on that expedition. She could see herself marching up into the foothills of the Himalayas. Definitely. Because she wanted things to change. Things to be different.

But radiator or not, she was slowly getting there. She was approaching the other of her own two towns, the place that counted as the end of the earth to the stay-at-home bods of Grenville—among whom she now sadly had to include old Cheryl.

She was coming from three days spent in Grenville with this old friend; three days which had turned out to be more than enough. She had stayed with Cheryl Dixon, thinking that they could renew a friendship and laugh like once upon a time, only to become frustrated at the way the new baby had given them so little time together. In confidence she had been told the pregnancy had been unexpected—not that Cheryl seemed to be put out in any way.

Cheryl was obviously quite satisfied with her life; with having moved to Grenville, and married the son of the stock agent, and entered the baby-making business. She had turned into such boring company; the suggestion that she come back to Robertson with Emma for a couple of days she treated as if she was being asked to take a canoe down the Limpopo. And to think that only four years ago her friend had been the epitome of sixth-form rebellion.

She was beginning to think it was time to stop wasting her uni vacations in these parts, family or no family. But she had grown up in Robertson; her parents still lived here ... 'The best of times, the worst of times ...'—something read in school. The worst of times for who? For a person who was beginning to hate studying economics, and whose radiator was leaking, that's who ... Certainly not for Cheryl.

It was a little after ten when she finally crawled into town. She drove slowly down the main street, playing her game of spot-the-changes. She liked to do this whenever she came down. Today she was not disappointed. Not only were there more and uglier car and caravan yards, go-ahead Robertson, she saw, had even acquired a Kentucky Fried Chicken joint. The whole town was beginning to get that rural–urban look, not unlike the outskirts of Sydney which she had passed through a week ago.

The old E–Z Motor Garage was still in place thank God. Thinking how good it was some things never changed, she smiled at Mr Stimson as he waved her through the mock Spanish archways of his establishment on Carlisle Street. Here, she had to fight off a barrage of questions about what she'd 'been up to of late', about the 'big smoke' and so on. But she did at last manage to get across what was wrong with the car. When he said she would have to leave it overnight, she set off to walk the four hundred metres into the town proper, to the studios of 2LBF Robertson, where she was meant to meet her father at the end of his morning session.

She walked quickly, hoping not to bump into too many of the people she knew. As a result of her father's fame in these parts, she too was a bit of a local celebrity—something which had always made her feel uncomfortable. But whereas Col Sinclair was involved in 'communications'—as he liked to term it—owning the local station, as well as performing for it, Emma Sinclair had gone off in an entirely different direction. She had gone off to 'do Economics'.

Her parents' acquaintances, the mums and dads of the kids she had grown up with, didn't seem to know how to take her anymore. Whenever she was back, they were always polite and inquiring, but she felt they missed the little Emma who used to play with their Belindas or Cheryls or Robbies much more than the girl who had gone all 'independent', and who blew into town these days only for a holiday—and that in her own car too.

She was half-tempted to take a wander through the shops, maybe say hello to Mr and Mrs Woodruff who ran the newsagency and were always kind to her. But she felt herself to be a little too disagreeable or irritable or something for the small talk she would have to make. She kept going, threading her way finally through the people exiting Fossey's next door to the station. She wheeled around and faced the doorway, then gathered herself for a leap that took her the three steps up into the foyer of 2LBF.

Inside, she found Judith sitting behind the switch desk, reading a magazine. She called out 'Hi!'

Judith looked up, pulling her cardigan into place.

'Well, well, the boss's daughter,' she said, in as unimpressed a manner as possible.

'He's got you behind the switch today.'

'Here and everywhere else, Emma.'

Emma was put off by the awkward, bored grin which next came over Judith's face. She was certainly not one of those people you could talk with easily. Nor did she ever seem to have much to say, content always to repeat that she was too busy being the Jill-of-all-trades around this place to indulge in idle chat.

'Is he finished yet?'

Judith suddenly and impatiently leaned across to a small panel on the wall behind her and turned one of the knobs. The sound of Col Sinclair's voice began to boom from the speakers mounted along the wood-panelled walls of the foyer.

'What does that sound like?'

Ignoring Judith's archness, she began to nod in a 'what we girls have to put up with' sort of way. She really couldn't work out why her old man kept Judith on. Why did he have to have someone as brittle and resentful as her, who was always acting like a martyr as well? She took a glance at her whenever she wasn't looking; hidden behind that make-up and a hairstyle that looked like a wig, she was just plain weird. But then little old 2LBF was such a small business, she supposed it was hard to get people who would do all the jobs that Judith did.

She decided to sit in one of the two armchairs across the room from Judith. Her father was into the last five minutes of his Harvester Hour of Old Favourites, and so she waited patiently as 'Stand By Your Man' droned to the end.

And then her father signed off with '... and that was Tammy Wynette with her hit of some years ago. A message in that for all you girls ... That's it from me for today folks. Until tomorrow when I'll be bringing you the Sales Roundup, this is Col Sinclair wishing you all a good day and take care.'

She had only just begun to get up from the chair when her father bounded out of the studio and into the foyer. Wheeling around theatrically he threw his bulk towards her, and the next thing, she was being cradled and carried around the room as if she were a baby.

Good old dad was obviously still in his performing mode. He began shouting 'Here she is! Here she is! Daddy's little girl!'

She didn't resist for a time, on the assumption that he would get tired of this silly game and put her down. But he just kept going around and around. On one of the spins around the foyer, he whisked her past Judith's desk, almost underneath her nose. The expression she caught sight of on Judith's face made her struggle more seriously.

'Dad! Put me down, will you? Put me down!'

He found a new way of tormenting her by kissing her

on the cheeks, and she once again saw Judith's face. It was set and stony, and trying to hide anger. Her father saw it too, and stopped for a moment to give her his full attention.

'What's the matter with you, Judith?' he said tightly, 'This is my daughter, you know.'

While he was diverted like this, she was able to pull free. She headed straight for the front door. Whatever it was that she had just seen, she wanted to get right away from it. She called out as she ran—

'Meet you outside Dad. See you later Judith.'

She had caught her breath by the time he came out to join her. From the change in his appearance as he exited into the street, she was pretty sure he had had words with his employee.

'What's up Dad? Something wrong?'

'No honeybunch, nothing at all ... Gee it's good to see ya! Come on ...'

And now he was pulling her by the hand along the street and around the corner in the direction of the car park. Between pants he shouted—

'We're going to have ... a special lunch for you Emma ... tomorrow ... because you're special ... Mum'll be putting on a spread ...'

So with dear old Dad, as far as Emma was concerned, nothing ever changed. As she looked at the side of his head, yelling back in her direction, she felt like laughing and she felt like crying.

She busied herself carrying things to the dining table. The others were in the living room. Her brother and her father were having an animated discussion in there; something about the quality of bush candidates in federal elections. A boring subject if ever there was one. Even more boring, and a better reason for keeping out of it, was the fact that Judith was in there with them as well. She had no idea why they had invited her to this, which was supposed to be for her alone.

Her mother was in the kitchen, and with each trip in there came a new lot of instructions—'... and the butter knives ... and put some peppercorns in the grinder, the pepper's in that cupboard ...' With the questions she had in mind to ask about Judith, it was annoying being diverted like this. What was more, she didn't like the way her mother tried so hard on occasions like these to coopt her, to fit her into the women's business. It was impossible to get through to her at this time—was there ever a time?

Taking her apron off, her mother turned to her—

'Call them to the table will you? I'm going to the bathroom.'

So she went to the door of the living room and called out as blankly as she could—

'Come on everybody.'

She stood by as the others arranged themselves around that old familiar table in that old familiar way; her father seating himself at one end, her brother on one side of him, her mother down the other end. This was where she herself usually finished up, with 'the proper space between the boys and girls' as her father always liked to say for humour's sake. The remaining space at her mother's end was today filled with the addition of Judith.

Along with her mother's placing the food on the table came something else familiar—the dreadful tension over who was going to serve what to whom. To cut it off before it became too involved, she stood up and began to ladle the contents of the casserole dish onto everyone's plates.

'Whoa! Enough!' her father called out, 'I can't eat that much. I'm getting to the age where I'm supposed to watch my weight, you know.'

But almost before he had stopped protesting, Judith came in with—

'Oh nonsense, Col, you still look fine.'

The warmth and indulgence with which she spoke surprised Emma. It was such a change since yesterday. There was something weird in the way she was so familiar. She tried to recall how Judith used to relate to her old man, say a year ago. But there was nothing to recall; he never used to mention her. She was always, as far as she could remember, just someone there in the front office of the station.

Her brother suddenly got up with a look of shock on his face and pointed at the food.

'It's still moving!'

He turned to his mother and grinned then. But the only one who was amused was her father.

Soon enough, and predictably, young Steve got Dad on to his tales from family history—stories he seemed to save up for the dinner table, and for when visitors were around.

He was a city man really.

Grandad came out to start an estate agency.

He was seen as progressive.

Country people were slow to take to new ideas.

In starting his own radio station, he was carrying on the tradition of enterprise established by his own father.

Things were beginning to boom around here.

And blah this, and blah that.

The shits already. She was amazed at how little time it took for them to give her the shits. Looking at her father sitting there all cheery grin and teeth and red hair and that big body of his, she felt like screaming. God how she hated how big he was.

She concentrated on eating instead, and decided to cast herself adrift. As he kept rabbiting away, she left for the Victoria Falls. That seemed like a nice alternative, a nice place to be. She imagined what it must be like to stand in the spray and mist of the cascades—a cool cloud you could lose yourself in.

But then her brother called out to her—

'Good to have you home, sis.'

And her father as well—

'Indeed it is.'

She hoped he wasn't going to ask her opinion about something he'd just said—whatever he'd been saying in the last minute or so was just a blank.

But her mother prevented that possibility.

'I was wondering when you lot were finally going to welcome her home.'

To this, her father replied, his voice dead and cold—

'Now hang on, Fiona. We're obviously glad she's home. And I'm sure she's not offended that we haven't put on a floor show for her … Are you Emma?'

'No I'm not,' she said, taking a quick glance at Judith, who was herself looking furtively at her mother.

She saw there was malice on Judith's face, no question of that. But she was also trying to clear her face of expression, as if she didn't want anyone to notice. As for herself, she hoped her own feelings were less obvious; she was certainly working hard at hiding them.

'But maybe,' her father added sunnily, 'maybe you're right in a roundabout way, Fiona. We haven't let the girl get a word in …'

'It's alright. I don't have …'

'You know, I was meaning to ask you. How do the Twin Towns look to you these days? Being away for a while, seems to me, gives you a good chance to judge. How are things in Grenville, for instance?'

'God, you should know, Dad. It's only twelve kilometres down the road.'

She shook her head in frustration; a gesture which was countered by a serene and patronizing smile from her father.

'Now, now, daughter, you don't have to get stroppy. I don't have as much time as you to get around. Besides, economics is supposed to be your line these days—I would have thought there was plenty for you to analyse around here.'

He paused for a moment to rearrange the knife and fork on his now empty plate, then began again—

'If you want my opinion, I think we're outstripping our cousins across the way. Robertson's turning into a real little go-ahead place.'

'I disagree. As far as I can see, things are just getting very tacky around here. Everything's tacky. Grenville is still a Bluebird Cafe town, and Robertson's turning into a Kentucky Fried Chicken town. That's the only difference, if you ask me.'

'Ha! Very professional! ... But then you always did like to exaggerate. Truth is, things really aren't that bad. Yes, we have had some imports, but I'd say they only help to liven the place up a bit. The bush will always have something. The people. There's a bit of cheerfulness you don't get in the big places. You can't tell me we don't have that.'

She pushed herself up and away from the table.

'I'm going to get the sweets. You want to show me what there is, mum?'

Her mother dutifully got up and followed her into the kitchen.

Once inside, Emma went and leaned against the fridge, folding her arms and trying to calm down. She watched as her mother brushed past and headed straight for the workbench. There, she lifted the tea-towel covering a cardboard box stamped all over with 'Matilda's Cakes—Robertson'. Her mother had never been much of a pastrycook.

'What kind is it?'

Her mother didn't answer, but took a knife and, leaving the cake still in the box, began to slice it ferociously.

'Nothing changes around here, does it Mum?'

Again her mother was silent.

'Mum?'

This time she turned—her eyes seemed to be damp—and was about to speak when Steve came in. He was carrying the dirty dishes.

'Here I am, mother's little helper,' he said, and made a show of getting out as quickly as he could.

Emma waited until he was well away.

'*He's* still the same ... Are you going to tell me what's the matter or not?'

Her mother gave no answer, but kept working; now putting the pieces of cake onto plates.

'Go on. Talk. What's wrong?'

'There's nothing wrong with *me*, Emma.'

'Are they giving you a hard time or something?'

'I suppose they are ... or he is ... or she is ... I don't know. What do I know?'

Emma went over to the workbench, not sure that she had heard right. She turned her mother gently so she could see her face. She had got it right, there was no mistake.

'You're kidding! Oh mum, you're kidding ...'

'I thought I could put up with it until it passed, or

whatever ... And he says they're finished, but she's still around, he still brings her here ...'

'Jesus, I'm sick of coming back here. I really don't know ...'

She made a move for the back door, but her mother caught her arm.

'But what about this dessert Emma? You can't go now.'

'I'm not going to eat *sweets* for God's sake ... How can you have ...? Tell them I've gone to see about the car or something. I'm going for a walk.'

She pulled her arm free and the next moment had opened the door. When she was through and about to pull it closed behind her, she called out at the top of her voice, unconcerned as to who might hear her—

'Why do you let them? Just tell me for once, why do you let them?'

She didn't go home that night. After walking the two kilometres down to the parkland behind the reservoir where she spent the rest of the afternoon with the ducks and the swamphens, she caught a lift back to town on a Shire truck. She then booked herself in to the Traveller's Rest Motel just up from the garage in Carlisle Street. God only knew what was happening, or going to happen, with her parents, but she was sure of this at least—she didn't want to be around if and when anything did happen. She had rung them, however, to tell her brother, who answered the phone, to apologize on her behalf—she had suddenly remembered she had promised to see Wal Stimson about the car, had been buttonholed there by an old friend, and would be staying over at the friend's place. She would be dropping by in the morning to pick up her bag and see them before starting back for Sydney.

She left the motel a little after nine for the short walk to the E–Z to pick up the car. She felt a little guilty. Not for having departed the way she had yesterday afternoon, more for having had such a peaceful, restful night's sleep. Aren't you supposed to feel something, upset or concerned or something, when your parents are behaving like complete idiots and you just run away? Nevertheless, there was no way she could have gone back into that dining room yesterday and played dumb.

She crossed the driveway apron to the pump where Mr Stimson stood filling someone's tank.

'Hello Wally, how are ya? How did you go with the car? is it fixed?'

'Good, good. Yeah. Everything's done. New radiator hose and cap, I put in it. But it's paid for. She's waiting out the back in the parking lot. Go and bring it here and I'll put some petrol in it.'

She went out to the lot, thinking that he'd made some mistake, got his invoices mixed up or something, and they would sort it out while it was being filled.

It was on its own in a back corner, facing the wall—old Wally couldn't have been doing much repair work these days. But it wasn't ready after all. She could see a head, tilted downwards—the mechanic she presumed—in the front passenger's side.

Only when she put her face to the driver's side window could she get a clear view of who it was.

Her mother.

She opened the driver's door and got in, readying herself for a blast about the way she had been behaving. But her mother, having lifted her head—she was holding the copy of *The Snow Leopard*—just stared in front of her.

'Listen mum. I know I should have ...'

Her mother cut her off, saying—

'Don't talk Emma. I didn't feel like it yesterday, and I don't now.'

'But what are you doing here?'

Her mother, instead of answering, ran her fingers across the buttons on the radio. She was very calm, no less relaxed-looking than she herself was, having awoken this morning in a neat and clean and strange room where someone had brought her breakfast on a tray. And then Emma became aware of something confronting and exciting here, like turning a corner on the coast road and suddenly getting a huge view of the sea. Her mother looked like she was ready for something; she was wearing make-up, her hair was done, and she wore a summery dress.

'I've paid for the repairs ... And if you look in the back seat'—Emma did so and saw suitcases, her own and another one—'I'm ready to go when you are.'

'You're not. I mean, are you? Really?'

'I am.'

'Where?'

'Sydney first ...' she smiled, tapped the book on her lap, and now, for the first time, looked at her daughter, 'then how about Inner Dolpo?'

Emma couldn't help it—she shrieked—and twisted herself round, the easier to throw her arms around her. But her mother saw what she was about to do, and leaned away, towards the window on her side.

'No. Not yet. When I've got it all right and worked out.'

Her mother became expressionless, which frightened her a little. She had always expected this sort of thing to be done with lots of heat, with explosions or something.

Her mother nodded in the direction of the ignition switch—

'Go on then.'

Emma started the car.

'Oh and by the way, Old Wal fixed the radio for you. You can get other stations.'

Emma poised her finger over the button—

'Do you want to listen to it?'

'Not fussed really. Your father's doing his Sales Roundup about now. I wouldn't mind knowing what lamb's going for today ...'

PARTYING ON PARQUET

He sat there on the edge of the bed, now gazing down at his new boots, now staring in the wardrobe mirror. Only a half an hour before people were supposed to arrive, and he was beginning to feel sort of paralysed. All these questions kept coming up, like the one with which he was currently grappling—one candle or more than one candle. Of the necessity for candles he was certain; but as to how many, he had no idea.

He wished he could ring someone. Theo maybe, yes, Theo who had been going to East Sydney Tech for years—he was someone who would have been to a million parties of the kind he was about to throw. Too bad that right at this minute Theo was somewhere in Cyprus on holidays with his parents.

He was new to this business of holding his own parties; there were a million other questions he would have liked answered for him at this moment. For instance: how much grog do people drink? He had bought some—beer and cask wine—but was it enough?

Then there were the dips. Because these seemed to be a pretty regular thing at parties, he had bought some from David Jones earlier in the day. He remembered that they had still to be taken out of their packets, and the crackers too. This practicality worked to mobilize him at last, and he got up to go to the kitchen.

On his way there, he pulled himself up in the hall at the doorway of his little living room and looked in.

It all seemed so bare. He had been renting this place for six months or so, had even accumulated a few pieces of furniture and so on, but this room still felt so empty. As did the whole flat really. Here, another little flame licked up around him, the fear that he might never be able to make it look or feel right, like a home that is.

But, as his father had said, if you leave your parents, you're on your own. Tonight, that was exactly how he felt.

He went through to the kitchen and opened the fridge. The six different dips in those little plastic containers with the houndstooth check took up most of the top rack—and what with the three wine casks on the bottom, and a few bits and pieces like sliced cheese and some carrots and a bottle of Coke, the mini-fridge was practically full. This food-buying caper was something else he wished he could get on top of.

He took the dips out and lined them up on the kitchen table. Using a teaspoon, he began emptying them into the soup bowls, the ones his mother had given him when it had finally sunk in with her that he was actually going away, leaving home.

They said he would get lonely, but he didn't feel himself to be *that* alone. He had made a few friends since moving out; it was they who were supposed to start arriving soon—Marina and Pavlos, and Penny. Penny—who was tutoring him in HSC English—had asked when he had rung to invite her if she could bring *her* friends, Jan and Greg. So there was every chance that he would soon be making some more.

He arranged the dips up his arms and headed for the living room. Once again, he stopped at the doorway and looked around. Was this the place to hold a party? It was so small; how many people could you fit in here? But these aside, the one question for which he desperately wanted an answer in advance was—would Penny like it?

Crossing into this room, he suddenly found his boots making an almighty clatter on the parquet. He put the dips down quickly and sat on the edge of the sofa to inspect their soles. What was wrong? These R. M. Williams had cost top dollar. There was nothing to see, but annoyed at this new development he put the boots back on the floor and began to test them for noise again. The soles weren't the problem, it was the heels. Weird because even though they didn't have metal tips or any-thing, they still made a sharp racket.

Back at the job in hand, he turned to moving the dips around on the side table, trying to find the best arrange-ment. And yet he couldn't help thinking about the floor. He had never noticed it to be so noisy—but then no-one had ever walked across it in big heels before.

The only solution he could think of was a rug, but it was too late to go looking for one now. He should have sorted this one out earlier. But how could he have known? This was the premiere outing for these boots. The only other way he might have found out was if he'd had a girl wearing big heels in here some time in the past. But this evening in fact would be the first time that chicks, booted or otherwise, had ever crossed his threshold.

What the hell. Penny was a uni student; she probably wouldn't give a stuff about such a silly detail. He chided himself for being so neurotic. As for Marina and Pavlos, they were only dumb ethnics like himself whom he had met at Greek dancing class; they wouldn't even hear the noise.

Again, he checked himself. There was no point in being defensive. This was his—this flat in a three-storey walk-up—and it was more than a lot of twenty-year-old guys had. What's more, how many of them had their own private coach, paid for out of their own wages? He found himself smirking, but then there was guilt.

With the good-looking Penny, whose ad in the local paper he'd answered at the beginning of the year, and whom he was paying—when he cared to admit it to himself—almost a quarter of his accounts clerk wages, he was rapt. He was well and truly gone on her, but it was, just the same, one big secret. It was a secret he had done a great job of keeping, even from her.

It was the first thing they said. The very first bloody thing. Penny and her friends had already arrived and were sitting there on the sofa. Pavlos walks in, with Marina right behind, Marina in *clogs*. And she says, 'Jeez your floor's noisy!'

Then Penny says, 'Actually, I was wondering about that myself.' And then she turns to Jan and gives her a knowing look and says very quietly, 'We're partying on parquet tonight, folks.'

And Jan starts giggling and says, 'Very swish.'

As for Greg, Greg who turns out to be a sarcastic bastard, he just starts making snorting noises.

He was pacing around the living room. He'd already taken all the leftover junk and dirty glasses into the kitchen, but was putting off the washing up. He couldn't help going over the things that had happened, playing them through his head over and over again. How could it have turned into such a fucking disaster?

Then someone had said, he couldn't remember who exactly, 'Hey! Where's the grog?'

So he went and got two of the casks, a red and a white, and the glasses as well. He put them down on the floor where Penny and friends were now sitting (Why did they do that? It seemed like a low-class thing to do)—and Phil says—'Christ, how many were you expecting?' Then Jan looks at Penny and then his way and hits him with—

'They're a bit big for wine, aren't they?'

Smart-arse Greg then asks—

'They're not from your Dad's milk bar are they Steve?'

This, *everyone* thinks is funny, even Marina and Pavlos, and they all start to laugh like idiots.

Penny's friends turn out to be not the sort of people

you can feel comfortable with; Marina and Pavlos never exactly relaxed with them, that was for sure. But after they've had this laugh, Marina, stupid Marina, gets up a bit of courage—she never usually talks out of place, why tonight? and says—

'So this is your tutor, ay Steve? Very nice. Very nice. Does your father know she's a girl?'

Jan starts raising her eyebrows and doing funny things with her eyes. But Penny pretends—he just knew she was pretending—that she hasn't heard what Marina has just said. Pavlos, good old Boilermaker's Certificate Pavlos, has to ask—'How much do you cost? Like if I wanted to come to you, how much would you cost?'

What he felt like doing at that point, he didn't do; and he was hating himself for it now. He wanted to tell them to shut up. He could have said, 'Why don't you embarrassing ethnics just shut up?' But he didn't, and that was that. Maybe if he had, they wouldn't have gone on. Maybe they, Pavlos that is, wouldn't have started talking about parents.

'How come your old man puts up with you mate?' he said. 'I mean, if I moved out, mine would shoot me. What does yours says about it?'

'Wow Steve, you're brave I reckon,' Marina tells him.

Hearing this stuff got Penny started, worse luck. God how it got her started. Thinking about it now was actually making him feel peculiar in the guts. She said something about how it must be very difficult living in a patriarchal family set-up, with a father of that typical kind or something. And then she had a gentle look on, and even touched his leg.

But at least he could see now he had got it all wrong. She just felt sorry for him—that's all it was. He should have worked it out from the way she just went straight on talking, even after she had touched him and he'd tried to get a bit closer to her there on the floor, with all that uni-type language and stuff about sex roles. If he'd seen then that she was only taking pity on him, he probably wouldn't have gone on to make a fool of himself later in the kitchen.

What followed all this stuff? Oh yes, everyone sitting around looking at each other and not speaking, until Greg asks if there is any music.

'Music?', he could hear himself replying, sounding surprised. The most obvious thing in the world for a party, and he, dopey Steve, had forgotten all about it. 'No, not really. Only the cassette radio. It's in the bathroom, hang on, I'll go and get it,' he had said.

But Greg said, 'Don't bother. We'll probably have to go soon anyway.'

He finally stopped the pacing and threw a punch in the air, imagining that bastard was there to collect it. It was just after midnight and enough was enough. He made himself head for the kitchen, with an idea that washing up would get his mind off the crap that went down here tonight.

He squirted detergent into the sink and watched the suds grow as he filled it with hot water. He wasn't very good at blocking things out anymore. Used to be, when a stuff-up happened, he would forget it straight away, just rub it out and keep moving. But as he got older, things seemed to hang around longer.

Piling the dirty glasses into the water, he knew it would take him weeks to stop thinking about what happened in here.

Still, he tried to go easy on himself and put his behaviour down to the grog he had drunk. He had got the wrong idea earlier, and the grog had just helped to make everything worse. What other reasons were there for cornering her in here, and blurting out that she was really great, and trying to grab hold of her?

The way she pushed him off—he hadn't expected her to be that angry, or that strong.

So what more did he expect?

The fact was, he realized, he was always expecting too much. And assuming too much as well. He hardly even knew her, for Christ's sake; it was just too soon to have done a big number, any sort of number for her.

'It's not on this level Steve. I mean you're a nice guy and all that, but as far as I'm concerned, I'm helping you with your HSC English and Maths. Right?'

'Right,' he'd said. 'Right, right ...' and backed away and bumped his head on the cupboard.

He pulled the glasses out of the water and put them into the rack. The rest of it could all wait until tomorrow. Wiping his hands on his trousers first, he turned the light off in the kitchen. But before he left there, he grabbed a glass. He would have a last drink to help him go to sleep; whatever he had drunk this evening had stopped working long ago.

In the living room again, where he stood filling his glass from the cask still on the side table, he changed his mind. What he really felt like doing now was taking a shower. His clothes stank from the cigarettes they had all been smoking, but that wasn't the reason. Something about washing it all away—if he could just wash everything away ...

He threw his clothes off there and then, and went straight to the bathroom and into the recess. Unlike at home, here you could have a shower without worrying about leaving water for somebody else—and there was no doubt he was going to let the water run right through tonight.

He turned the knobs and got into position.

It was magic, just letting the water run down his body—the best thing that had happened all night. No soap, no nothing; he leaned against the tiles and watched the steam begin to slowly fill the room.

Yes, living on your own had a lot of things to it unlike home.

For all that tonight had been such a mess, there was no way he could ever go back. You didn't have to get in early at night. You didn't have your crazy father waiting for you to come in, and giving you a look up and down.

And smelling you.

That trick of his of coming over and smelling around him, searching for something. Grog? Perfume?

What would he have done if he'd ever found anything?

There was no use in even mulling over it. That part of it was all over; what he had to do was learn how to cope with this new deal.

Well, at least one problem could be solved, the Marina and Pavlos problem. That was simple—they were out. Finished. No more. He didn't need people like them to make him look stupid.

And he would apologize to Penny.

As for Greg and Jan, the only way he would ever be able to get on top of smart arses like them was to beat them at their own game. He would study hard and get into uni. He would throw that stuff of theirs back at them so hard, they wouldn't know where to duck ...

After a few minutes, the heat started to get to him, exaggerating his tiredness, making him sleepy.

He looked at his skin, going red in different patches on his shoulders. The steam had got so thick, he could hardly see a thing. He stared up at the ceiling. It was hanging there like a mist, a fog, with the light shining through; and it was his for as long as he wanted.

ONLY IN THE TRUTH

In the end, Peter took the plunge and invited Jilly over too. Because he had split up with her four months ago was no reason to think she wouldn't be interested in his new project at least—as a matter of fact he could recall telling her his plans for this one while they had still been together. Certainly, *he* was over the traumas of the break-up, such as they were; and they did have more than a little in common, workwise.

He had told her about Sonya, who would also be coming, as neatly as possible the last time they had got together for a cup of coffee. That she had taken the news of his new lover so well—without the slightest reaction actually—and that she had been heard to remark to a mutual friend she was feeling a bit lonely these days— these he took as hints that she might even enjoy a night in their company. As for the material he had gathered already, he was sure she would appreciate it.

He was pleased with the way things had gone so far tonight. Sonya had organized the food—a tray of lasagne which she had brought with her by taxi to everyone's amusement, and which had turned out to be just delicious. Really, the only cause he had for concern was that they had taken the whole two hours from seven-thirty to demolish the food. This was holding up the main proceedings a little.

But by standing and hovering over them at the table, and trying some animal herding noises—which made them laugh—he did manage to get them out of the dining room and into the living room. Here, the fire he had lit earlier was into a pleasant, burning-down phase. Waving a bottle of Chardonnay around, his finger over the opening, he pointed out the seating possibilities.

The bottle he held was their third, started late during dinner and so still more than half-full. Nicely loosened as he was, as he thought they all were, he made a little thing of counting heads.

'Sonya yes, Jilly yes, and me yes ... Yes, we're all here. I never thought I'd get you out of there.'

Jilly, who was arranging herself onto a cushion on the floor, said, 'Well, we're all here now. When does the show start?'

'As soon as I top everyone up.'

He pushed the bottle of wine out in front of him and then leaned over with it to fill their glasses. First Sonya, who had chosen to sit in one of the armchairs, then Jilly. As he filled his own glass, he eased himself down into the other armchair, next to Sonya and across the coffee table from Jilly. From here, the cassette player on the table was within easy reach.

Hanging on to his glass carefully, he reached forward and put the bottle down on the table with a small flourish to signal that the preliminaries were over.

'Right. As you know, Jilly, Sonya and I have finally be-gun working on this oral history project—researching the experiences of postwar migrants ... Sonya suggested—and I think this was a good idea—that we start close to home, with my own parents ... So to cut a long story short, I decided to interview my mother and ...'

He stopped when he saw Jilly smile. 'My God,' she said, 'you didn't! Did you?'

'Yes I did. And the best way to do that I thought ... the best way to do that would be to have a really clear struc-ture—you know, chronological questions, certain sub-jects, and so on ... but it was very hard to get her to stick to it, and so I finished up just asking her the odd ques-tion and letting her talk—you know, random thoughts, whatever she wanted. The idea being we could put it into context later on ... And now without further ado ...'

He reached forward again towards the coffee table, to press the start button on the recorder.

'By the way, we've done some work on the beginning of this already. My first question or cue or whatever you want to call it has been edited out, and this is Sonya's voice you can hear reading my English translation ... I began by asking her about my Uncle Tassos. There was a big fuss about his death when I was a kid, but I never knew the details except that he was killed ...'

He pushed the button. A moment later, Sonya's voice began.

'They buried him at Botany Cemetery on the side sloping up to the oil refinery. I wanted them to put him nearer to the bay, to the water, but there was very little room left there. It was too much money in any case. If only we'd had the money, he could have been away from those tanks and towers and pipes ... and those lights at night, God, those awful orange lights out there ...

'I didn't write home to tell them, to tell them that my brother, our beloved Tassos, had been killed in Australia, for over a month. The months after that were an awful time, a black time when I thought over and over again of my own death, of bringing it about somehow so I could go and join him in peace ...'

Peter went for the pause button.

'I should say here before it goes on that at this point she asked me "why?" Why did I want to bring all this up again twenty-five years after it happened. I left that out of the translation.'

'Christ,' Sonya began, 'I know what she means about those lights though. Have you ever been out there at night Jilly? It's ghastly.'

Feeling that Sonya had deliberately changed the subject, Jilly said, 'I take that to mean, Peter, she's saying it's none of your business or something—if she asked you why.'

'There's no such thing as "none of your business" with the Greeks, Jilly. One person's business is everybody's business. No, that was just my mother's sense of drama and tragedy—"we are wounded and we will never heal", which is very Greek too I suppose ... anyway, then I said I don't remember the details, you never told me the whole story of how Tassos died ... this is what she said.'

'... It's not easy ... it's not easy, but you are a man now, you should know these things ... Alright. When your father was not doing any good in the hardware shop, I went to work for Prevelakis, in his clothing factory. We argued, your father and I, but I had to go out and he knew it— what else could we do to get money?'

'It was alright there, well not too bad anyway. Some nice girls, some gossips. The boss was, Prevelakis was, what can you expect? He played the *effendi*. We always had to check our pay, keep count of our hours or he would try things. It never happened to me, but he robbed some of the other girls ...

'I met a girl—she wasn't that young, she was thirty-five, same as me. She was from Kythera. You might remember her name, I'm talking about Sophia. We talked and we liked each other, and after a time we became such good friends, sweet friends. And we still are. After all that has happened to her, to me, we still are ... after all that they did to us we still are ...'

After a pause of a few seconds in the tape, Peter pressed the stop button again.

'What's up?' Jilly asked him. 'She was just about to get into it, I thought.'

'Well, I cut out about a minute's worth here. Unfortunately she became a bit emotional. I left the gap out of respect, I suppose.'

'Do you think we might be able to hear the rest of it without any more interruptions?' Jilly asked archly.

'Now, now, all things come to those who wait, you know. And by the way, we did eventually get into a question and answer format—but that's further on.'

He put it on fast forward for a moment, but because he overshot the beginning, he had to fiddle awkwardly, running the tape back and forth until he could find where it started again. Sonya had become a little agitated through all this, but as for Jilly, she seemed not at all fussed. She was content to sip her wine, and to the extent that a contribution was necessary, to smile benignly.

He finally got it right.

'I told her about the new church in Leichhardt, and why doesn't she go there instead of going all the way to Kingsford every Sunday. That's where we go now, I said, my husband and I, and my brother ... and you, little Peter. Come with us, and bring your brother too if you like. Bring Stelios ...

'How many times I've thought of those words since ... What can I tell you? I could see it happening right from the first, from the first Sunday they saw each other. It went the way these things go. They began to see each other. Tassos started to come to the factory—he used to say just to pick me up after work, but this was just his excuse to see Sophia.

'And then he would go to her home in Lewisham, to visit her there. That's when the trouble began. Her brother began to object—she used to tell me at work the day after. I knew when it was happening. Stelios wouldn't come home until late at night, the next day Sophia would be at work looking upset, sometimes red-eyed ...

'"Stelios was angry at me again after Tassos left", she used to say, "He shouted at me." And then later, once or twice, she came to work with a black eye, or bruises on her arms ... It was terrible, and it was getting worse.

'I told Tassos many times to be careful not to cause trouble, to understand that Sophia's brother wanted to protect her—she was a single woman after all. She had no parents, no relations here but for her brother. It was natural. Your father too, he used to say the same things to him.

'But for Tassos, everything was alright. There was nothing to worry about, everything would be fixed, he was beginning to win her brother over ...

'Then one night, something happened; they had an argument in the flat, Sophia's and Stelios's flat, and Tassos came home in a rage ... I remember him saying how he was going to write a letter to Sophia's parents in Greece, to tell them what was going on, how he intended to marry her, and how badly her brother was behaving ...

'I never realized until that night how serious it had become between my brother and Sophia. Then ... the next time Tassos went to visit her, one or two days later it was, that was when it happened. What can I tell you ... Stelios followed him home. In an alley, a back street, he took the gun he was carrying and shot him ... he shot my brother ... Not a hundred metres from here, his home ...

'I found out the same night, because Stelios told me himself. He came to the door and told me that night. He was crying like a madman. He threw himself down at my feet in the doorway ...'

Peter stood up this time, and with a look of concern now pressed the player into fast forward.

'Sorry folks ... same as before. But that's the end of that episode anyway.'

But before it had run on very far, Sonya said—

'Stop it there for a second Peter will you ... I know we talked about trying to somehow use all the material we got from your mother ... But this first is much more moving than what follows, don't you think? Maybe we should just scrap the rest of it.'

'Hey, hang on,' Ely called out, 'I haven't heard it yet. Give us a chance.'

Peter said, 'Yes, but she might have a point there.' He then looked at Sonya rather seriously. 'We can talk about it after Sonya ... Now, the mellifluous male voice you will next hear is me. I ask the questions and Sonya, as always, pretends to be my mother.'

'I was wondering what you were doing for one these days, actually,' July pronounced.

'Watch it!' he retorted. 'No cheek please.'

As he prepared to start the tape again, he managed a furtive check of Sonya's face, looking for a reaction. There was none. She seemed not to have heard, which didn't please him all that much. He had an idea he was beginning to need an ally. If *she* wasn't to be that, then who was there?

'Here goes ...'

'Tell me, why did Father buy a business so soon after you got here? It was more usual to go and work in a factory, wasn't it?'

'He was proud, that's why. He wanted to be his own boss, and not have other people tell him what to do. He was stubborn ... What a Big Boss he turned out to be! He only had me to give orders to!'

'*You talked earlier about going to work in the factory and started to say what it was like there. Can you remember anything else?*'

'About the factory? What is there to remember? It was hard work, long hours, the usual things, nothing out of the ordinary.'

'*What about the union, did it help? Was there someone from the union there?*'

'No, there was no union. But why do you ask me these questions, you who went to university. You should know how things are in the world, without asking your silly old mother.'

'*I'm going to do many interviews like this, with people like you, so that we will have enough material for a book. We want to put these injustices down on paper so that there will be a record, so that such injustices are never done to the migrants again.*'

'Injustices to the migrants ... Peter, if you want to know who did the worst injustice to me, I will tell you straight. It was your father. That's who it was ... He used to say he was the head of the family, the breadwinner, but I still had to go out and work when the money was low. And after coming home from work, I still had to cook and clean. He never helped me. He would go out and play cards ... or visit his girlfriends ...'

Peter pressed the stop button, this time with an air of finality. He spoke tightly—

'That's it. I called it quits there with the interview.'

'Why?' Jilly asked.

'She just launched into an attack on my father. There didn't seem much point in recording a whole tirade of nothing but personal bitterness ... And in the final analysis, she's only one interview out of what's supposed to be twenty or more ... And I'll say this—when she starts on my father, I refuse to put up with it any more. She just heaps abuse on him. She's not the saint she paints herself to be—I know what she's like ... It's not the sort of stuff I'm interested in.'

He turned to Sonya with a kind of childish, wounded look and asked—

'I mean, are we?'

She touched his arm from where she sat, gently and soothingly.

'I don't think so, Peter. No, we aren't.'

As if a load had suddenly been lifted from him, he grinned and got up slowly. He took the bottle to fill their glasses, but saw that it was empty.

'Wait here you two,' he said, moving away towards the kitchen, 'I'll go and get some more.'

'Good,' Jilly called out after him. 'Yes, let's have some more grog.'

She also stood up, thinking it about time to ease the pain in her back. She began to stretch, bending her body from side to side, then touching her toes, once, twice, three times.

Sonya gave her a little round of mock applause and said 'Well done Jilly'. And Peter came in to find her reaching her arms over her head.

'Well, I'm pleased to see *someone* is still doing their exercises.'

As Peter took up her glass to fill it, she lowered herself onto her cushion again. She had a slight sheen of sweat on her face, which she wiped away with her fingers, and she was slightly out of breath.

'That fire's making matters worse ...' she said. She studied the glass of wine he had just poured for her and made up her mind she would not drink any more tonight. To stop drinking was important for another reason—she had one or two things she was sure now she wanted to say. Just for starters, she thought of this one—'... but I still think I'm fitter than either of you two.'

In that Peter heard—he was absolutely sure—the good old unmistakeable Jilly malice. The bitterness in her was *the* fundamental flaw in her character, he had always said—and to her face as well. This was what, in his mind, had driven the wedge between them, had just plain turned him off her.

'And to that I will add, in *every* way.'

'What are you talking about Jilly?'

For all that he was a little bit drunk, it was hard to miss that other familiar feature—belligerence. Yes, he had got her number long ago.

'Look, there's something I have to say about this tape

you've been playing—not to put too fine a point on it, your intentions are immoral.'

'What? When?'

'In this plan to leave out your mother's "personal bitterness", her "abuse" or whatever you called it. How is that stuff any more personal than her feelings about the death of her brother?'

Sonya watched Peter as he tried to get an angle, to find a form of rebuttal, but he seemed to be struggling. Being unconvinced herself of the wisdom of inviting Jilly around, she found her own reaction confusing; a mixture of feeling justified, and wanting to protect him.

He ended what looked like a period of contemplation with—

'You've got to have principles of selection.'

'If I were you I'd leave the whole lot in. That way you can't be accused of a perverse form of censorship. Indeed, I'll make sure the charges are dropped.'

'Now come on Jilly, this isn't my mother's memoir or something you know. This is using oral, *oral* accounts to build up the ... sociological picture.'

'Oh is *that* what it is?'

'What's with you anyway? I have to tell you you're sounding a bit nasty old girl, bitter almost.'

'There's that word again!' Jilly shouted. 'As I've told you a million times before, that lexis, to borrow from your ancestors, only describes effects and symptoms. You, however, insist on using it as a weapon in your moral armoury.'

Peter turned to Sonya and said, confidingly—

'It's the brog, I mean grog.'

'Look who's talking?!' Jilly fired back.

She was amazed to see Peter and Sonya begin to laugh, for all the world as if someone had farted or slipped on a banana skin. The nervous idiocy she saw in them prompted a giggle of her own. For the moment at least, the something not-altogether-pleasant that had taken hold was eased. But then there was nothing except silence.

Peter began wiping his lips. He was thinking how he was willing to admit to himself that he had made a mistake with Jilly—having her here tonight was in a long line of them. But it was surely the last one he would ever make with her.

Sonya, who had an idea she should try and restart the conversation, came over and sat on the arm of his chair. She began by saying rather loudly—

'I think your mother's account of that death was moving, I really do ...'

'You said that earlier,' Jilly interjected.

'So I'm saying it again, do you mind.'

'Girls! Girls!' Peter tried to make it into a little joke. But he succeeded only in tipping Jilly over the edge.

'Stop being stupid, Peter. I don't like the way you're turning out I'm afraid. All this oral stuff ... oral–anal more like it. That gap "as a mark of respect ..." Why don't you try pulling the other one? The bits you finally choose for this book or whatever will be the ones that suit your own advancement. You're clever enough to know which ones they will be, I'll give you that. It's your own ambitions we're talking about here aren't we?'

'For Christ's sake Jilly, what are you talking about? I happen to be genuinely concerned ...'

'Genuinely concerned for your own future might be a better ...'

'I think I've been wasting wine on you,' Peter cut her off with as much of a snarl as his slightly numb lips would allow. He went on—'I had an idea you weren't really over our breaking up.'

While he spoke, Sonya had the terrible idea that they were both, in different ways, and for different reasons, trying to get at her. She had no other way of explaining what was happening. She had never seen Peter behave like this before.

'Do I have to hear you two argue?'

'Why not, Sonya? It's your turn to put up with him it seems.'

Jilly then quickly gathered the cassette recorder up, pulled the cord out of the socket, and sat there holding the machine to her chest. She felt like a little schoolyard fun. She began rocking backwards and forwards and stuck out her tongue at both of them, knowing well enough that she was driving Peter into a familiar corner, familiar to her if not Sonya as yet.

'You're just using this ethnic bit, mate.'

'Don't you tell me what I'm using. Unlike yourself, I'm interested only in the truth. I happen to care very deeply about ...'

'Ho, ho, ho, don't make me laugh. Where would you be if you didn't have your migrant heritage to trade off? You're just lucky you lot are in favour at the moment, sport. Which leads me to say you're just a product of the times, and your dirty need to be somebody.'

At this, Peter stood up from his chair.

'I think you'd better leave.'

'Sure I will ... but not before I call you an upstart as well.'

She took up her glass and raised it as if proposing a toast.

'Ladies and gentlemen, I give you Peter Dracopoulos, parvenu Greek!'

Peter marched towards her, planning to grab her by the arm; but by the time he was in a position to do that, she had leaned away and in a flash had taken the cassette out of the player and thrown it in the fire.

Distracted, Peter immediately lurched towards the fire, followed an instant later by Sonya who had jumped up from where she sat. Peter pushed her back, shouting 'I'll get it! I'll get it!'

Using the fire tongs, he reached in and got hold of the cassette. He was unable to pull it clear of the still-alive embers before it had begun to melt. When he did get it out, he swung around on the spot, holding the molten plastic mess to one side of him, and aimed a look of anger and outrage at Jilly.

Jilly, however, saw it only obliquely. She was already up and away, looking for her coat.

Sonya approached Peter gently and got him to put the cassette and tongs down on the tiles in front of the grate. They embraced in front of the fire, both drained, both tearful with a new love for each other.

She put her hands on either side of his face.

'Don't worry darling. You know we've still got the transcript. No harm done.'

SINGLE LENS REFLEX

The way Dom had been buggerising around the studio all day it was giving Alfio the shits. Just because Dom has a day off, don't mean that *everybody* can down tools. Something was eating at his cousin and Alfio could tell.

Alfio was in the darkroom putting fixer in the tank. But the door was open so he could look out into the studio and see what he was doing every so often. For the last little bit he'd been watching him drag a pair of studio lights around the floor in front of his backdrop sheets.

Next second, he's turned ten thousand watts on. He shouted at him through the door—

'Jesus, Dom! What are you doin'?'

'I want to light the wall so it don't get shadows ...'

'Who's gonna pay the electricity bill? ... Know what I reckon? I reckon you've got a chick problem, Dominic Manzetti. You're not gettin' enough jiggy-jig ... But I dunno why, there's heaps of it around here ... The place you go every day. The Tech. There's chicks laid on down there—and I do mean *laid* on ... So what are you waitin' for?'

To say something, Dom answered—

'The right one.'

It didn't sound right, he realized. But he always found it hard to answer back to Alfio who was always so sharp.

He never felt real easy when Alfio was going on about birds either. How can you compete with a guy who'd taken photos of chicks with no clothes on?

'Oh mate, that sounds to me like mama's talk. If I was you ... What are you doin' down there, did you say? Tell me again, I forgot.'

'Mechanic.'

'Oh year. Dom's gonna be a toolie.'

Dom hoped Alfio wouldn't start going on about his apprenticeship—he already knew that his mate reckoned it was bullshit being an apprentice. Sure he didn't want to be a mechanic; he wanted to be a photographer same as Alfio. That was why he spent most of his time hanging at the Biondi Studio in Crystal Street—he wanted to pick up on how to do it. But he had never told Alfio that.

As far as Alfio Biondi was concerned, they were just cousins. If he'd known Dom's real reason for coming in here every day, he would have told him to piss off. He had enough problems. Just to make the dough to call himself a photographer was one. And when things went wrong—like yesterday's wedding stuff—he had no time for anybody else.

Earlier today he had developed the B&W's he took at the reception—the colour stuff he had sent away to the lab. There was a hassle with exposures. The lighting had been poor in that Venezia reception joint, but he thought he'd compensated right. As it turned out, he was going to have to spend extra time fiddling with the prints to get them up to something OK.

And then there was the crap he had to put up with on the night—not just last night, for Christ's sake, they were all the same ... 'Ey! Mr Photograph! Put my face in the pitcha! No forget, ah? In the pitcha with Maria! How much you say? Quanta Costo? Five dollars?! Aoo, too much for justo one.'

For a long time he had wished this wedding stuff, and all the other bread and butter work he had to do, to the shithouse. He was sick to death of it—the way everybody always wanted to haggle. What he wanted to do, deep down really wanted to do, was glamour and fashion work.

'Peasant!'

He shouted this as hard as he could, startling Dom into dropping the light filter he was trying to fit. Dom picked it up and faced Alfio, expecting another blast.

'No, not you, idiot. This jerk. Come and have a look.'

Dom entered the darkroom as Alfio finished washing one of the prints he had managed to save so far. He held it up in front of his cousin with a pair of tongs, pointing to a man standing beside yesterday's bride in front of the church.

'Look at him. This fat shit here ... father of the bride ... Jeezus he give me a hard time.'

Dom nodded sympathetically.

'Listen mate. I give you some advice for when you get a job. If they start calling you *goumbah*, you duck. That means they want something for nothing.'

He pulled a few more prints out of the wash and began hanging them in the drying cabinet.

'Hey! You still here? Better get goin' or your old man's gonna start ringing me up.'

Dom turned to go without another word. He didn't want to overstay his welcome, he didn't want to muck things up now that he was starting to get the hang of the basics. He was at the back door almost straight away, and opening it said—

'See ya, hey can I come on ...'

But before he could finish, Alfio had his answer.

'Listen. Stop comin' around here every five minutes. Go and get some jiggy-jig, will ya. It'll relax ya! Ha! Ha!'

Dom tried a little laugh too, and not wishing to offend, closed the door behind him.

After he'd gone, Alfio gave a thought or two to the possibility that he was being a bit hard on Dom. But no, business was business, and there was good reason to clear the joint early tonight. He was expecting someone.

Last week, this guy had rung out of the blue, wanting to know if he was available for some glamour work. When he'd said 'sure', the guy went straight on and said he'd be around on Monday night to talk about it some more. It seemed a bit weird that he didn't want to give his name, just telling him he was an art director with an advertising company. It was as much as Alfio could get in to tell him that he'd done plenty of nudes—'chicks want to be models, see'.

He had been wondering since whether the bloke believed him. But with Dom out of the way now, he could get on and do a bit of groundwork. Because you can't take anything for granted, he thought he'd leave a bit of his earlier stuff lying around—some slides, some prints—for this art director to look at. If you didn't blow your own trumpet ...

He hadn't got very far with trying to choose slides on the light table when he heard the sound of a car in the back lane. It was a big sound, V8 or something, nothing like the locals' cars. Then it pulled up and stopped. He went out to have a look.

He wasn't disappointed—it was a Porsche. And there he was for sure, the man sitting in it. It had to be. That's the sort of cars those guys in advertising drive.

It wasn't until he was out of the car that Alfio got a proper look at him. He couldn't believe how young he was, not much older than himself, maybe thirty, and wearing red trousers and a cream shirt—the sort of gear he himself fancied, even if he couldn't afford it.

Alfio waved and caught his eye, and the bloke came up the lane to him. He didn't seem to want to shake hands.

'Are you Alfio Biondi?'

'Yeah, come inside,' he said, pointing the way in.

'Ahh, I'm a bit busy for that sport. Come and sit in the car, and I'll tell you what I want.'

Alfio did as he was told and followed him to the car—this would be the first time he had ever sat in one of these darlings.

Once inside, he couldn't help smiling like a big kid. These Porsches were just too much. He was aware, however, that the guy was giving him the once over.

'Do you like it?'

'I sure do, Mr ...? I didn't get your name.'

'Call me Mick.'

'Yeah, OK. It's a top car alright ... cost top dollar too I bet.'

Alfio ran his fingers along the dash and leaned over to inspect the instruments.

'I'll give you a good look at it later, Alfio, but what I want to know today is if you're ready to do some photographic work for us.'

'I'm lookin' for work, Mick, no risk. But you didn't say much about it when you rung me, like.'

'So I'll tell you now ... My associates and I, we run a studio out west ... We do sort of a lot of *glamour* work there ... well, we don't do it ourselves see, we just hire out the studio ... Anyway, what we want is someone to come in on a regular basis to lend a hand on the *technical* side of things for some of the, ah, clients ... It's three hours a night at thirty bucks, five days a week ... Interested?'

'Who are the guys doin' the photography?'

'All sorts of blokes, Alfio.'

'And like, what, are they workin' for advertising and magazines and that?'

'Some of them probably are, yeah, that's possible.'

'Right, right ...'

Alfio was silent for a while, as he put all this together. It was a bit different to what he'd expected; he had thought they wanted *him* to do the photography.

'Well, what do you reckon? The set-up is out at

Barnstaple.'

'Can you gimme a bit of time? Do I have to tell ya now, like? I wanna have a think before I say yes, or I say no. If you don't mind.'

Mick let out a sigh and grabbed the steering wheel with both hands. He tilted his head downwards and stayed that way for some time, leaving Alfio with the impression that he was a bit cranky.

'A think ... Alright. Tell you what I'll do. You can let us know tomorrow. And if you say yes, you'll be starting straight away. How's that?'

'No worries. If I have to start straight away, that's no worries.'

Mick leaned across him to open the door on Alfio's side.

'So I'll ring you tomorrow morning.'

Alfio got out carefully, conscious of the door lining and the possibility he might scuff it. He stood by the car as Mick started it, waiting to wave him off.

Back in the studio, he fell to doing what he usually did whenever he was agitated, or excited, or had something on his mind—cleaning his lenses. He gathered them all up off the shelves, took them out of their cases, and laid them out on the light table—24mm, 35, 43–86, 80–200 zoom, and his joy, the 300mm telephoto. He lined them all up in a row. And using a little kit he kept just for this job, he set to work to dust and clean them, beginning with the 24.

This he knew: things never turn out exactly how you want them. What he thought was going to be his first bit of work for an ad agency, he wasn't sure was going to be that at all. Not only that, it wasn't too clear just what he was being asked to do—just something about helping some other photographers with their work.

He twisted the aperture ring from F2.8 through to F22, loving the way it clicked at every stop. This was a beautiful wide lens—even if it did distort a bit at the edges if you pointed it down.

But that was OK. He could live with it. And he could do with the bucks—the eighty dollars rent he had to pay here every week wasn't all that easy to find. Eighty a week for the back storeroom of an old factory. It gave him the shits. Looking at it another way—whatever it was, it was work, and he would be getting his name around. In this game, getting yourself known was important, real important.

Next morning, he was all ready to pick up the phone when Dom, unannounced as usual, came in through the back door.

'Hey! It's Dom! Just when I'm gonna get on the phone.'

'Sorry. I'll go if ...'

'Nahh. Stick around. I got some news maybe you wanna hear ... Listen to this. I got some terrific new work, mate. Out at Barnstaple. Technical adviser I'm gonna be mate, technical adviser to some guys working for an agency. Real high-powered stuff. What do you say?'

Dom said 'Great!', and a moment later it entered his head there might be something in this for him. It was time he came out with his own little plan.

'Great ... ah Alfio ... is there anything maybe I can do there too? Tech is crapping me off and I've been thinking I wouldn't mind being ...'

'Sorry mate. Nothing else going there, I reckon. Hey, you never told me you wanted to do photography. That's why you been hangin' here huh?'

Alfio saw the look on Dom's face and beckoned him closer. He put his arm around his cousin's shoulder.

'But hey Dom. You got a lot to learn before you ready for this sort of stuff. If I'm tellin' you to piss off, don't listen, huh? You can come here when I got some time and I'll teach ya, don't worry.'

Alfio had understood for some time that he was Dom's hero in lots of ways. It tickled him to think he could affect other people like that.

'Now listen to this ...'

Alfio put on his 'aren't I something?' expression for Dom and with a flourish lifted the receiver to make his call.

'Hey yeah Mick, it's me, Alfio Biondi. I'm ringin' to say about that job, yeah—seven o'clock, OK, OK,—can you tell us about ...? OK, OK, see you there, see ...'

He was disappointed that he hadn't been able to ask the questions he wanted answered. He looked at Dom.

'These guys don't muck around mate ... That's how come they've got all the dough, and you and me, we ain't got any.'

He leant against the wall and watched the little fat guy trying to get his act together and take his photos. Three sessions tonight, two weeks so far, and he hadn't said a thing about it to Dom. And he wasn't going to. This, he didn't want anybody to find out about. The way things were going, he couldn't see himself doing it for much longer anyway, dough or no dough. It was getting on his nerves. Take tonight for instance.

Three new wankers he hadn't seen before. And no Mick to sort things out. There was never any Mick, he never came around at all, as far as he could tell. There was only the guy at the door who gave him his thirty dollars each night. So he'd had to put them in the waiting room and say who was going in first, who second, and who third.

These new ones, they didn't know the first thing about photography—not cameras, not lighting, not nothing. Just as well the girls were pretty patient. But even for them, sometimes it was too much and they'd start going off.

Talk about being fed a line. What he'd been given to do turned out to be nothing like what he'd been expecting. He shook his head at this one and tried to work out how much longer.

Seeing as how the cameras in here were all old and worn, he had brought along a single lens reflex of his own. But it was looking like that had been another mistake. He had put it on a tripod in the middle of this room, the 'studio', and preset everything. But the little fat guy was mucking around with the focus, turning the focusing ring this way and that, this way and that.

Debbie had finally got the shits with all the extra waiting and called from behind the screen—

'God help us. Isn't he ready yet?'

Even standing as far away from him as he was, Alfio was sure this one had never held a camera before in his life; he was also sure that all his fiddling had shifted the aperture ring. The photos would turn out like a dog's dinner. He'd come back to pick them up when they were developed and no doubt start complaining.

The aggravation was finally too much, forcing Alfio to join him behind the camera.

'Mate, what are ya doin'? It's all ready. I set it up before. Focus, exposure, lights and flash, everything. OK? All you gotta do is tell her what you want. And then you push the shutter.'

The little guy was starting to look a bit confused, and then he went a bit red in the face. He was obviously new to the game. Alfio had had enough.

'Look. You paid your dough, didn't ya? Now this is what you do ... Debbie? Come out will ya?'

Debbie, who was short and thin, maybe seventeen or eighteen, came out from behind the screen. Alfio had a lot of time for this one—even if she was a redhead and skinny—and so he always went a bit gentle with her. So far, he'd never had to tell her to take her clothes off either. She was always ready.

She went and sat on the edge of the couch.

'Open your legs love.'

She did as she was told.

Alfio took the little man's finger and put it on the shutter. He pressed it down. The shutter clicked, the flash went off.

'See mate? It's easy. It's a single lens reflex. Nothing to worry about. OK?'

PERFECT HOLIDAY SOUNDS

She had been gazing at the man on the beach for quite a while. Sitting in the sunroom at the back of the house, she had become frustrated with the *Beautiful Homes* magazine she'd been reading—it was full of the sort of glitzy inner-city interiors she hated—and had looked up and out over the garden to the curve of the beach beyond their fence. That was when she'd first noticed him, but from the sweat on his body—or was it oil?—he must have been there for some time beforehand.

He was very thin, and yet had that low-hanging sort of belly that said old, and even from this distance she could see the wrinkles and folds of aging skin. He was walking around in a small circle, perhaps five metres across, now taking huge, slow strides, now mincing little steps, and all the time flapping his arms up and down like some demented bird. An albatross on its last legs, desperately trying to get airborne one more time.

But the amusement was starting to wear thin for her. It was absurd for an old man to be carrying on like that. She pushed her chair into another position so that, while she could still look through the glass of the sunroom doors, she wouldn't have to look at that particular character.

They had been here five days, there were only two to go before they had to get back, but she had yet to relax fully. Was it the weather that was causing her to feel so irritable these last few days? It had been patchy, with clouds and showers and only a few hours of sun every day. This, according to Dennis, was to be expected. It was the second half of May. More likely it was all due to the usual end-of-term tiredness. Add to that the strain of moving in and setting up this holiday house in such a short period, and it made a bit more sense.

It wasn't the *buying* of the place that had been so difficult, but rather the problems of organizing another household two hundred kilometres from home base in Sydney. She wished, moreover, that she could be convinced that taking this Blenheim Beach cottage was as clever a decision as Dennis had been making out. For years he had talked about a place to get away to when the brats of Year 9 had become too much to take, and now he had such a place.

Maybe it was only a matter of getting used to it here. It was a pity they only had two more days. A little longer just might have seen her into a better frame of mind.

She got up to go to the front of the house to find Dennis.

She pulled open the screen door to the front yard, and there he was, raking leaves off the driveway.

He saw her in the doorway and said, 'Thought I'd get the cleaning underway ... So it's no big deal on the last day ...' He pulled the rake a couple more times, making a loud scraping noise. 'Ah! Listen to that. A bamboo rake across brick paving, one of those perfect holiday sounds ...'

'If you say so,' she said. 'Just remembered something I meant to tell you ...'

He stopped and straightened up to look at her properly.

'Remember that woman who runs the fish market? Mrs Kellet? Remember how she mentioned she knew our neighbour on the corner down here? The one with the cats ...? Well, I met her this morning when I went down to the beach store ...'

'Oh yes, so what about her?'

'Well, she's got cats alright ... dozens of them, all over the place. She introduced me to her champion, this big, huge thing sitting on the verandah by the name of Bernie—bigger than a wombat it was. You should have heard her. What a clever, wonderful thing it was, and all her other cats that she has to feed and look after because nobody else around here will ... and so on and so forth ... And then they wonder why there are so many feral cats about and why the bird population is declining ...'

'Amazing, isn't it,' he said and went back to his raking.

'Oh, and the other thing was, she said if we ever want fish to go down to Kellet's fish market. I told her I'd already met the good lady, and she replied "Small world isn't it? I sometimes get sardines for my pussies there." True, that's what she said, "I sometimes get sardines for my pussies there ..."' She finished up with—and rather ominously he thought—'It *is* a small world down here though, and a funny one too ...'

'Funny alright. But it's a real community too, don't you think?'

'Hmm,' she said.

He saw her turn and move into the shadow beyond the screen door.

'Let's go for a walk later,' she called to him.

They had left it a bit late, so that by the time they got down to the sand, the wind had picked up. It was an agitating wind, pushing in from the sea, blowing her clothes around. She turned to him and said, 'You're the expert on winds. What direction's it coming from?'

He worked out an orientation from the position of the sun, low behind the broken clouds to their left.

'We're heading north. So it's northeast. A typical afternoon coastal sea-breeze ...' and then mocking a television weatherman, 'typical for this time of year, folks.'

She quickly paced a few steps ahead, swung around to face him, and said, as childishly as she could, 'Thank you mister ...'

'Just call me Dennis, little girl!'

She laughed and took off running.

She ran for what felt like ages, but, looking back, saw she had gained only fifty or sixty metres on him. After she stopped, she occupied herself looking for sea-shells until her breath came back, and he could catch up with her.

After a time, he appeared, jogging, by her side.

'Hey ... about improvements ... Let's make a list ... Hey? What do you reckon? Tonight?'

'If you like.'

They kept going until they reached the end of the beach where the rocks began and inclined towards a small headland. Neither of them was in the mood for climbing rocks. To their left, there was an opening in the scrub. They looked through the gap in the vegetation and saw what looked like a billabong or a small lagoon, its runoff to the sea blocked by the spit of sand on which they were standing.

When she saw what she thought was a path, along the water's edge and heading inland, she grabbed his hand and squeezed it.

'Let's go up along the side there ...'

She tugged at his hand but he didn't seem interested. She let go of him then and set off anyway, through the long grass growing on the soft earth along the banks.

He watched her tramp away until she was out of sight. There was nothing up there, he was sure. Although he didn't want to be left standing around here, it was only when he could no longer hear her moving through the undergrowth that he set off after her.

He had never been up this stretch, but he could quite easily tell what it would be like. The vegetation, which was thick enough to start with, would eventually get thicker, and soon enough impassable; and with all this water under a cloudy autumn sky, the atmosphere more dank and unpleasant.

Hemmed in by stripling gums on one side and the water on the other, the only path was the one he could see she had taken, over the mushy grass and reeds. He did not have to go very far, however, to reach the place where she had come to a stop.

She was standing at the edge of the water, looking down.

'I wish you wouldn't scamper off like that all the time ...'

She didn't answer him, but waited until he was next to her before pointing down at the water.

'Look at that,' she said.

The channel was narrow at this end, a couple of metres across, and full of stagnant, yellowish water covered in some sort of film.

'So? It's not running. That's what water gets like when it can't run.'

Pointing again, she directed his eyes to the bank on the opposite side.

A concrete pipe ran down the slope and through the bushes to the water. The end of it hung over the bank, and from the opening, a slow stream of foul-looking liquid fell into the lagoon.

She asked apprehensively, 'What is it? What's that stuff coming out over there?'

He grinned.

'Don't you know?'

'It's not, is it?'

'Probably ...'

She put her hands on her hips and shook her head in bewilderment.

'Don't worry about it. It's probably treated somewhere first. They wouldn't let it run into this backwater like that otherwise.'

'It's criminal,' she said angrily. 'Just criminal.'

'I told you there was nothing up here, didn't I?' he said, and turned to go back the way they had come.

Lacking the motivation to organize a proper dinner tonight, she had allowed herself to be conned into takeaway. When he arrived back from Terry's Beach Store with some awful-looking, greasy white packets, she was not sure it had been the right move.

He went straight into the living room with them. 'Come on. Let's not fuss. We can eat on the floor in front of the TV ...'

He arranged the packets on the floor and then more or less pulled her down beside him onto some cushions.

'This is called going all the way ...'

He opened the wrappings. He had bought a barbequed chicken and some fried chips.

'Do we really have to eat this rubbish,' she asked.

'Of course,' he replied, and theatrically pulled the wing off his half.

She could not for the moment bring herself to eat any of this, and watched him instead as he gnawed away in that meticulous way of his. Pretty soon, she had an urge to distract him. It was something she had never got used to, the way he ate.

She said, 'Hey, slow down! Aren't we meant to talk tonight about what we're going to do with this place?'

'That's right!' he said, 'So we were. So we were ...'

He put the bone down and tried to wipe his hands on the edge of one of the wrappers.

'Oh Dennis, for Christ's sake. Go and get a towel.'

He did as he was told. But when he returned from the kitchen, rather than sit down again, he went to the old gas heater in the corner of the room.

He pointed an accusing finger at it.

'This has to go, for starters.'

'Why?'

'Don't you remember? Old Spooner said it doesn't work.'

She thought for a moment; yes, the old boy *had* mentioned the heater. 'Does it *have* to?' she said. 'I love that sort of one, and you know how cold it can get down here. Can't you make it work?'

'Are you kidding? Getting these things going when they're in this state is a real art. I can do a lot of things, dear girl, but fixing this is beyond even me ...'

She tried to force herself to eat something, but could get nowhere with it. She got up off the floor.

'Hey! Aren't you going to even try?'

'I did try. I'm not hungry, as it turns out.'

She left him still sitting on the floor and went to the bedroom instead.

She lay down on the bed and began a relaxation

exercise. She was concentrating on releasing the tension she could feel in her arms when she was startled by a series of hammering bangs coming from the living room. She threw herself off the bed to go and see what was happening.

In the living room, Dennis was still on the floor, but had moved to be sitting in front of the old heater. He had pushed the chicken scraps and take-away wrappers into an obscene heap in one corner. He was holding a hammer.

'What are you up to?'

He put one hand on top of the heater and gave her a sheepish look.

'Just thought I'd get started with this ...'

She thought a dose of sarcasm was in order, but was saved the trouble. They heard a voice at the door; someone was calling out 'Hello! Anybody there?'

'More noise ... You go out, will you Dennis.'

She was in no mood for visitors.

He put the hammer down and left the room.

She moved a couple of steps closer to the door and then stopped, so she might hear who it was. She heard a heavy, male voice say 'Evening' and then Dennis repeating the word. It sounded odd, listening to him take the lead from someone like that. He never used that word himself. She felt a bit frightened. She couldn't hear very clearly what was said next—something about 'a good idea to check'—although she was relieved when that heavy, older voice broke into a couple of laughs. Again, she heard Dennis follow.

Then he called out, 'Kate?'

She went to join him at the door.

He had pulled the screen open and was welcoming a very large middle-aged man and a very large middle-aged woman inside.

'Come in, come in,' he said and turned to her. 'Kate, these are the neighbours we haven't met yet.'

They both smiled at her and said 'Evening'.

'Hello,' she replied.

'We're the Lockharts from next door,' the woman said.

Dennis led the way into the living room. 'Come and sit down,' he said, pointing out the arm chairs.

This pair didn't seem interested. They went to the centre of the room and began to look around, the woman especially, at the walls, the furnishings, and so on.

The man turned to her and extended his hand. 'My name's Hugh ...'

She put out her hand to have it engulfed by his. Then he said to her, 'I heard some bangin' before and I just thought I'd come and investigate. Been away a couple of weeks ourselves. Didn't know anyone had moved in yet.'

Dennis said, 'I explained to Hugh that I was working on the heater, Kate ...'

The woman took this as a cue and began, 'Mmm, I can see that ...' Then she turned to her husband or whatever he was. 'They've made a lot of changes already, Hugh. The Spooners would never recognize it now, would they?'

'No, they wouldn't love,' he answered her.

The woman looked at her directly. 'You young ones today seem to like a lot of rugs and cane chairs and bits and pieces. Don't you find they gather a lot of dust?'

'Well ...' She was going to say 'not as much as you might think', but the woman turned away abruptly to go and inspect something on the side table.

While she was there, bending over and peering at one of her favourite pots, she said, 'You don't seem to have kids—have you got kids?—which gives you more time I suppose ...'

'As a matter of fact,' Dennis said, 'no, we haven't got any kids ... yet.'

This was as much as she wanted to take. She turned quietly and went to the kitchen. She was damned if she had anything to say to anyone any more.

After she'd been a few seconds in there, on the edge of tears, the idiotic Hugh said 'We'd better get a move on love'. Dennis moved them past the doorway of the kitchen. 'The Lockharts are going, Kate ...' he said, with the suggestion that she ought to say something.

She said nothing, only to hear him top it all off with, 'She's not feeling very well tonight ...'

By the time he had come back inside, into the kitchen, she was weeping freely.

'Don't you talk about me like that ...'

'What did I say?'

She clenched her fists and glared at him as fiercely as she could. 'I hate those people! I hate them all! They're all so *old* down here! It's for geriatrics here Dennis! Geriatrics!'

When she had calmed down a little she went and sat at the breakfast bench.

She said, flatly, 'I want to go home where I belong ... And I want to have kids ...'

He came around behind her and put his hand on her shoulder.

'It's a holiday house Kate. A weekender, that's all. We're not going to be living here ...' He began to stroke her hair. 'You're just a bit overwrought ...'

As a contribution towards helping heal last night's injury he had volunteered to do most of the cleaning today. There was sand to be swept off the mats and floors, and a bathroom to be scrubbed, and all this he had done willingly. As a further contribution, he had suggested they drive the twenty kilometres into Nowra tonight and have dinner in a proper restaurant. It would be nice to partake of at least one of their city rituals he knew she enjoyed—dinner out on a Saturday night.

'We may as well treat ourselves,' he said to her in the car. 'It's back to school on Monday ...' It seemed an extra pleasant thing to do on this particular night. The wind had been blowing all day, not just a sea-breeze, but strong and cold from the south.

It took hardly any time to get to Nowra, they saw at most five cars along the way. An additional reason, he thought but never said, why Blenheim had been a good choice. In the town itself, they reconnoitred from the comfort of the car. There were quite a few restaurants, enough to allow some choice anyway, and after driving up and down the centre of town and along the three main streets a number of times, they settled on what looked to be the least pretentious, the Sung Ming—Chinese and Australian Meals.

To avoid walking any further than was absolutely necessary in this cold, they parked as close as they could to the place.

Once inside, the feeling he had looked forward to was delivered. The warmth was fantastic. He looked at Kate and saw she was smiling and that was good. He squeezed her hand while they waited to be seated.

A table was found for them, and the waitress had gone away for menus when he thought to play a little game. He got her attention by touching her on the arm, and said, 'The pattern's begun to shift ...'

She reacted not at all, which led him to think he ought to continue to go carefully with her.

'Alright, I won't tease,' he said. 'I mean the weather pattern has started to shift—the highs have begun to move to higher latitudes and those old winter southerlies are starting to come back ...'

She replied with, 'And so are your old obsessions.'

He didn't mind her saying that; she appeared to be joking.

Something like twenty minutes passed before the waitress, a very thin girl of, she estimated, no more than fourteen or fifteen, arrived with the menus. The contents of the menu itself did nothing but reinforce for her that they had probably made a mistake in opting for this place. She ran her eye down the headings—'Pork', 'Beef', 'Chicken', 'Chow Mein', 'Australian' ... and said, 'Hopeless isn't it? So suburban ...'

'Oh really Kate ...' he replied softly, 'Does that matter?'

She chose not to answer, but to try and make the best of it. She had already concluded that she was not feeling all that wonderful again this evening.

With the food that arrived what seemed like hours later, she could make no headway whatsoever. It was glutinous and too salty. He noticed that she wasn't eating and said, 'Your appetite looks to have disappeared down here, Kate ...'

'It's not my appetite that's the problem.'

She decided she could only cope with the boiled rice.

'Never mind love, we'll know better next time ...' he said, and again touched her hand. 'Have you thought about what we should do with the house? By way of repairs, I mean.'

'No, not really,' she said, and made one last attempt to swallow some of the beef. 'Besides, what do I know about hammers and nails and things ...'

'I can think of a few little things, nothing serious though. Those loose floorboards in the kitchen, that hole in the bathroom wall, and the doors, the doors in the sunroom ... did you notice how they don't shut properly?'

'No I didn't.'

'They're not hung properly.'

'Is that so?'

She was beginning to tire of this gambit of his. He was being stupid. He knew she didn't know the first thing about repairing things. And she had no desire to learn either. She thought of her girlfriends who had taken up that sort of thing. With them, it never got very far; some neurotic striving for a few months. He wouldn't let her go somewhere to learn anyway. He would want to teach her himself.

What was of more immediate concern was how truly awful she was feeling. The longer they sat in this place, the more diabolical she saw it to be. It was dirty; *all* the waitresses, not only the one who had served them, were under-age and couldn't give a damn about what they were doing. And why should they anyway? They were only kids. And overhead, hanging from a garish lantern, was a strip of flypaper. They were still using flypaper, for Christ's sake.

Her anger had caused her to stare up at it now where she had noticed it only casually earlier. This time he was aware of what she was doing.

'What are you looking at that for?'

'Can't you see what it is? It's flypaper ... That must tell you something about our taste.'

He studied it for a time, trying to imagine why it was making her so vitriolic. But he honestly couldn't see why anyone could get so upset about such a thing. He said, 'Come on, you're overreacting ...'

And that dreas it. In an instant, she was very angry. She glared at him and said tightly, 'I am *not* overreacting Dennis.'

'Isn't it a bit much to be worried about things like that? I said we'll know better next time, didn't I?'

She repeated 'I said ...' but could get no further. She stood quickly in her place, pushed her chair back, and headed straight for the door.

Walking away, she heard the sound of another chair scraping the floor behind her. She looked briefly over her shoulder and saw that he was following her.

They drove home through a long, black tunnel. Or that was how it seemed to her, sitting in the kitchen, staring at the clock. It was still only nine-thirty. She had her hands around a mug of instant coffee, trying to get warm. The remorse had set in almost as soon as she stepped out of that restaurant, but the drive home had somehow made it all worse. It had taken a mere fifteen minutes to get home; fifteen minutes, however, along a secondary road with no street lights, only those low, dark bushes hemming them in on either side.

That was something very disconcerting about Blenheim Beach. As soon as you went inland, the thick vegetation of the coast simply petered out and it became all flat and pathetic scrub.

The coast was an illusion. Maybe it was all just one big mistake.

The whole thing.

Just then, a banging sound. She couldn't believe he would do it, but it was happening alright. He had started hammering again. It made her frantic; the thought that he could do something like this so soon after a quarrel.

She could only think that this was on purpose. He was deliberately torturing her.

She jumped up and raced to the back of the house and the sunroom. There he was, sitting on the floor with the doors open in front of him. His tools were spread out everywhere, and, the same as last night, he had a hammer in one hand.

'Are you serious!?' she shouted. 'It's cold, damn you! It's cold!'

He said, quite calmly, 'That's why I'm trying to fix these doors, Kate. So they'll shut properly and stay shut ...'

She marched over to him and grabbed the hammer. She brought it back and swung it in a curve at the glass of one of the doors. The glass shattered. He ducked out of the way as the slabs fell to the floor around him. In the next instant, she let go at the other door. With this blow, she managed only a small hole in the middle of the pane.

She felt him grab her leg and then she was on the floor. She struggled to get up, but it was impossible. He let go of her leg only to straddle her and pinion her arms. No matter how hard she tried, he kept holding her down, using, she knew, all his weight and strength.

When she heard his voice, she wanted to block her ears, but there was no way she could move her arms.

He was shouting, over and over again, 'Kate! What's the matter with you? Kate! What's the matter with you ...?!'

THIS WIZENED CREATURE

My God James! Once I saw what was happening, a little devil got into me or something, and I began to play that nasty little girl's game too. I mean, I feel terrible about what I did *now*, but at the time I just got carried away I suppose …

Well if you want details … Actually there were lots of difficulties in the way of my getting the job in the first place—so it was really a fluke that I got involved at all. For instance, first time on the phone Mother was surprised I wasn't a *Greek* dressmaker. 'No dear, my name *is* Cleo but I'm not Greek … That's alright,' I said, 'We're both silly, I didn't know girls had debuts anymore either …' And honestly Jimmy, I didn't. It was a real experience for me, I can tell you. I hadn't done any sort of a debut gown for years and years.

But what I was telling you about earlier, the debacle, happened on the day of the fittings—before that, there were only a few sparks. Not saying I knew what was happening right from the beginning—I don't take credit for being that smart—but there were plenty of clues, thinking back on it. Although she asked me that first time whether I was Greek, you see, I never assumed *she* was. Her English was very good on the phone, and she gave her surname as Malley. But when I get out to South Coogee for the first session—South Coogee is a giveaway though, isn't it? So nouveau—and she opens the door, and my God, she's a foreigner of some sort, well ... Turned out her real name was Malios or something.

If I was *really* clever like you I would have been able to tell from the first day that something was going to happen. Mother and Daughter—daughter was about seventeen by the way—lead me into the living room, and there's old Granny sitting in the corner of the room, all in black, like something from a nightmare. And here I am, laying out my designs on the floor—on the shaggy pile don't you know—showing them materials and so on, and there's this gargoyle staring at me from the corner, never moving the whole time.

I thought that first session was going to be a total waste of time, because all Mother wanted to do was to make me cups of coffee and serve me sticky sweets—not that I objected to that, of course. And talk? God could she talk. But I was so fascinated, I couldn't help wasting time myself, just sussing things out. Mother tells me that Father is an important man in the Community—he owns a Factory—never did find out what sort—and that he is Very Successful. Well, he'd have to be, dear, I should have said, if he can afford *my* prices ... And then this business about her daughter's debut. So I came back with 'I didn't know ethnics,' that's what I said, I could have kicked myself, 'I didn't know ethnics went in for that sort of thing.' So Mother tells me the story and I sit there with my mouth hanging open ... 'Yes, they do, just like everybody else,' she says. Everybody else! Where have they *been*? Turns out they have something called a Greek Young Debs Ball each year! ... Now stop laughing James, it's true.

She even showed me pictures. Her other daughter, who's away doing medicine somewhere or other, got 'presented' a few years ago. There she was at the Wentworth with all the other girls—and wearing this dreary thing straight out of the fifties. When I saw that, I made it quite clear she shouldn't expect anything of that sort from me.

This daughter? The one I was doing my bit for? Well, she was quite short—they all were really, Mother and Granny included. But a lovely little face. Beautiful skin—they all seem to have such beautiful skin, don't they? Must be all the olive oil. Really, there was only one problem. This girl, young Efi, had the biggest boobs you've ever seen ... How big? I mean *big*. From the minute I first saw her I was thinking 'I hope she doesn't want decolletage.' Because we would have to get an engineer! Well, as I said before, those boobs were her mother's downfall. But that's the end of the story ...

No, no, let me go back a bit—I have to pick up the thread again ... What? Yes, I'm joking ... So Efi sits on the floor with me, in her jeans and sloppy joe. Just a nice little kid, I was thinking. And when her mother's done with trying to fill me with baclava and coffee, she finally sits on the edge of the sofa and starts to look down at my patterns and samples. She had a concentration span of about thirty seconds, did Mrs Malios. So what happens?

I tell them what I would like to do—something simple and tight, to pull those things of hers into line, cool colours, high collar, bit Mod-ish ... sort of no sleeves and hugs the bum, thank you very much. But Efi, she sees something from years ago I keep meaning to throw out, and decides to go all funny with us ... Now, I swear, before she said what she wanted she took a sly look, first at Mother, then at Granny. Then she says, bold as brass, she wants *that* one, the one that's above the knees, and with a plunging neckline. That's what she called it too, a 'plunging neckline'. Granny didn't budge—she didn't speak English. But Mother, oh yes, she reacts alright. I thought 'You little bitch Efi, you've done this to your mother before.' I'm sure if I hadn't been there they would have been at each other's throats. In the event, Mother manages to restrain herself.

But she's really got a problem now. She doesn't like my suggestion—she's still wearing pants-suits by the way, and with a body like hers—and she very definitely doesn't like Daughter's idea. She tried to reason with her then—silly person. It'll be too cold, you'll look like a tart ... and so on. I am a model of diplomacy of course and say nothing. And do you know what that little girl says to her mother? I kid you not, she says—'But I *want* to look like a tart.' God only knows what magazines she's been reading. Last year's *Cleo*s no doubt.

However, in the interests of peace, Mother passes over this and other remarks of hers, and in the end she gives in. Turns out it's been a battle to get Daughter to agree to be presented in the first place. OK. You can have the dress, as long as it's not red. OK, says Efi, and then they look at me ... What could I say? My financial situation, as you well know James, is not such that I can stand on principle all that often. OK, says I too. I'll do it. What the hell, so it's out of date, what do I care anyway. I can always salve the old conscience by tricking it up a little bit.

Then it's time to take the measurements. I get out my tape, but we've got another problem here. The girl who wants the daring dress happens to be shy about having her measurements taken, and she wants to do it herself. 'Don't be shy Efi,' I say, 'I'll have to know what they are if I'm going to make a dress for you, won't I?' But she's determined, and it's only when she realized she couldn't read the numbers upside down that she let me do it. Talk about having to work for a living! Honestly! Anyway, I get that job out of the way, I pack my things, and they lead me out. 'See you next week Mrs Malley. See you later, Efi.'

So next week comes around and I'm there again. In the meantime I've run up something for the little miss to try. But before we get to that, it's on again with the hospitality—she's never heard of too much of a good thing, that woman. Only this time it's worse because not only do I have to pretend to be eating ... hmm? ... those biscuits with the icing sugar, sort of a shortbread, I can't remember what she called them ... but I have to sit there and listen to her prattle as well. The poor thing, she was trying so hard to impress me, cynical old me, I mean, if I was her I just wouldn't have bothered. She told me what she had bought last week, what she was going to buy next week, that sort of thing. Someone should tell her—money doesn't buy class, now does it? They come over here from their villages or whatever, and the next thing they're *wanting* everything. I don't understand how they think—how can they be something they're not? A leopard can't change its spots ... I've got off the subject, haven't I? ... Oh yes, and while she's rabbiting on, Granny appears, with her crocheting, and goes and sits in the same corner as last time. We have to wait for Efi, because she's not home from school yet.

This waiting did give me a good chance to look around the living room though. In some ways it was hard to tell this lot were Greeks, you know. Take the furnishings for instance—take them? they should be given away. It was so tacky, if you know what I mean. There was this gigantic ornate sofa and armchairs, done in crimson velvet, and *drapes* hiding the windows, and those carpets I was telling you about ... and on the walls, on the walls she had those awful king-size pictures—there was a stormy sea on one of them, and I think horses, yes, just some horses on the other—the sort you can buy at chemist shops. But the only really *Greeky* things were these gigantic wooden worry beads she had everywhere. Now they *were* a giveaway—she had them on the coffee table, on the side cabinet ... The side cabinet, what a production that was! It had glass on the front and inside just dozens and dozens of goblets, big, huge copper goblets—the sort you can't drink out of ... Just hysterical.

Did I say anything? Not much. She never gave me the chance! Ummm ... I did ask her at one stage about how Father's Souvlaki Factory is going ... no, you fool, it's a joke, didn't I tell you earlier I never found out? And I did say something to her about my clientele, some of the more famous ones. She was all ears about *them*, I can assure you ... But finally Daughter does get home. She slams the front door shut and she walks into the living room—not so much as a nod of course—and straight through to her room. Absolutely no manners whatsoever. Mother calls out 'Efi! Efi! You come straight back in when you're changed!'

Eventually Madam Efi reappears and I can get down to work. Well, naturally, the thing fitted, but we still had to sort out a little problem, namely how much of Efi's ample whatsits we are going to expose. This subject took up at least an hour, mind you. Needless to say, Mother's all for hiding as much of them as possible—a hopeless idea considering the type of dress we had on our hands. While Daughter's idea is to hang them out all over the place ... I hope you're not getting the wrong idea, Jimmy. You asked me to fill you in and I am, no more than that—I certainly haven't got anything else on my mind ... And as for Granny, she's just sitting in the corner, casting her evil eye over proceedings, as usual.

Mother's telling her 'No, no, darling, at least *this* high,' but as soon as I've lifted it an inch, Daughter's tugging it back down again. Honestly, I haven't come across such a little minx as this one in a long time. Mother's getting more and more worried, 'what about your Father, it's his money,' but this just doesn't wash with our Miss Efi. I'm sure if I hadn't been there they would have put on a tremendous scene. Then I noticed that every little while Mother was taking a glance at the old woman. She would pull the dress up, catch Granny's eye, and just sort of stand there *looking* at her. It was only after she'd done it a couple of times that I worked out what she was up to. She was *checking* with her, checking with her own mother to see if it was alright. But Granny wouldn't budge, just kept sitting there with that glum stare of hers. What an evil genius that child was! She'd found this terrific way of tormenting her mother, and was going at it full pelt, *pulling* the dress down, having it lifted up, then *pulling* it down again. 'No, mum, I don't *want* it so high.' At the end of about an hour, as I said, Mrs Malios, poor thing, is very worked up—she's got the sweats and her cheeks are like little tomatoes, little red tomatoes.

But look James, I really should make my confession, shouldn't I? I let myself become a tool of that little person's, I really did. I don't know ... deep down I'm probably just as nasty as that little girl. Don't know what came over me ... perhaps it's just that I like rebels—I'm a rebel of a sort aren't I? Or Mothers ... when you've had one like my dearly departed, you can be forgiven, can't you ... But there I am in the end, actually aiding and abetting Daughter, and saying 'Yes Mrs Thingamy, I think she's right, it should be lower'—that's what I meant when I was telling you at the beginning that I was playing it for all it was worth—'yes, it *should* be lower ...' If I'd stuck to my principles she wouldn't have been in such a dress at all—and if taste were a consideration, well ... Funny thing, though, the whole thing had a momentum of its own.

Alright, alright, I'm getting to the finale, don't worry. So Efi had won the battle, or so it seemed, with a little help from this guilty sinner you see here sitting in front of you. I really thought it was over. I mean Mother was just a quivering wreck by now, and all she can say is 'alright, alright, if that's what you want, if that's what you want ...' And me, I'm resigned to going away to do the final work on this ridiculous dress, and I'm gathering up my things from around the room.

But all of a sudden, Mother turns to Granny, *yaya* I think she called her, and says something to her in Greek. I think she must have asked her whether she liked the choice—that was probably what it was about because, as I say, she'd been looking at her every so often through this ordeal anyway. Whatever it was, oh my God, the proverbial hit the proverbial! This wizened creature gets up, turns to Mother, and shouts such a load of abuse—I don't know what she said exactly but I know abuse when I hear it—in this screechy, high voice. And then she comes up to her, right up to her, and spits in her face. I'm not kidding, she spat in her face. I mean, I thought that sort of thing only happened in the movies, but no, there it was right in front of me.

And then this diabolical *yaya*, she turns around and walks quietly out of the room. All the time I'd been there, she'd never said a word, the same as on the first time I was there, only now, when I thought everything had been decided she lets loose, spits in Mother's face and walks off. What did this do to Mother? It *finished* her, that's what it did. It was the *coup de grâce* ... That's French, silly ... She fell in a heap on the sofa, and put her head in her hands and started crying, I mean *really* crying, bawling and howling. I'd never seen anything like it. It was pitiful, truly, truly pitiful. And meanwhile Daughter's just standing there, still in that dress, looking stunned, and staring down at her Mother. I don't think she could believe it either.

What did I do? Well, what can you do when something like that happens? The state she was in, if she was a dog you'd shoot her to put her out of her misery. I just sat down and put my arm around her shoulder and made soothing noises to calm her down. It was the least I could do. Such a terrible, terrible sight. A grown woman howling like that in front of me, a total stranger ... but then they are supposed to be more emotional than we are, aren't they? ... The Daughter? She clenches her little fists and she goes up to the door Granny left by and she shouts—'You always muck *everything* up, you do! Just *everything*! ...' As for the dress, that was the last time I went there. Never finished. I've kept it as a souvenir though. If you want to have a look, next time you're in the studio remind me and I'll show you. I've got it hanging up out the back.

TO MRS STARKEY

As I am just about ready to go, Mrs Starkey, I thought I should leave this note for you. As you know I have been talking about doing a trip for a long time. But I have been planning it too, which you don't know. This is very important to me, just like you have been. That is why I am leaving you this note. You have been more than just my landlady, more like you were my mother really. So here goes.

When you find this I will be on the road, heading north, I expect. My plan is to go around Australia by bike. You know how I have always been rapt in my bike, Mrs Starkey, well it is going to take me around the country. I have been thinking to explain what my bike means to me for a long time now. A lot of people do not understand what it is about, or how someone can ride a bike as much as I do. The thing is they know nothing about bikes, not as much as I do in any case.

Most people think all bikes are the same, just something with pedals you push around. But there are lots of different kinds, ladies' bikes, sportsters and tourers, and ones like mine, proper racing bikes. You should really be using a tourer for this trip, but a racer is lighter and anyway a twelve-speed like mine with a double-butted frame and the works is really the king of bikes. You get to know your bikes when you have been riding them as long as I have. Sixteen years, since I was fifteen. So what if I am a bicycle nut. It is nothing to be ashamed of to my way of thinking.

There has been a lot of new bicycle clubs started and a lot more people are riding them, but I think a lot of it is just a craze and the latest fad sort of thing. I hear the Institute has been on at the government for more cycle ways and parking facilities for bikes, but I do not think that is such a good thing. It is only encouraging a lot of people who do not really love the game to come in and push us real bikies around. There is too many hippies and lezzos riding around on bikes these days already. It is the 'alternative' types everywhere. Maybe it is true what they say, that bikes do not cause pollution and are efficient technology alright. But that is not the real beauty of them. Also, the social thing is not what it is all about either. Sometimes you see photos from the old days and there is hundreds of people in them, all from the same club. Women and men. It was a really big deal then. You can still be in a club now if you want to, but I have always kept out of them. Too much pressure, I reckon.

No, the real beauty of the bike is how it is really personal, you on your own. Riding a bike can give you freedom, and that is the most important thing. That is what I get from it. Before I had a bike I had no freedom, everyone was always telling me what to do. My old man. My old lady. You should have heard them going on when I was a kid. I am glad I went away from them when I did. They were no good to me, that lot. When I left them I was no good in myself for a long time, even though I got a job and had a bit of money. It was not until I got a bike that things started to get better for me.

But when you are on the bike you do not have to put up with any crap from anyone (sorry for that word, I know you do not like bad language!). You can just think what you want, or just watch things. You can ride and ride for hours and feel so free. Talking about watching things, that is what I am going to be doing a lot of on this trip. I planned out a really good route so I can see everything worth seeing up the coast. I should write GMH a letter and thank them. Best thing they ever did for me closing down that joint. I was six years there, and I have been six years here at Chelmsford St with you and the others. Funny how things work out. You should be coming with me. That way I would not have to worry about tucker, ha! ha!

I have got to watch my money on this trip, so whatever I eat it will be cheap stuff like hamburgers probably. I have been saving for a while and I have got enough I reckon. Also, I left you two weeks rent and a bit more so that you do not go bad until you can get someone to take my old room. The extra money I left is for the blanket I took. I already bought some stuff for camping out, but I will get some more for when it gets really cold at night. I am going to be sleeping out under the stars, which is going to be great.

In case you are interested in what I am going to be seeing on my way up, this is the list I made. It is only to Queensland because I do not know yet what I will do after that, or what there is up that way much.

Day 1—Get to Gosford. Have a look around town. Camp overnight.

Day 2—Newcastle—Steelworks—Camp.

Day 3—Forster. Camp on beach.

Day 4—Port Macquarie—fish.

Day 5—Coff's Harbour. Visit the Big Banana. Stay in motel overnight.

Day 6—Lismore?

Day 7—Murwillumbah—Border—

It is a pretty full trip at least until I get to the NSW–Queensland border. The furthest I ever went before by bike is to Gosford and back. I did that in the one day a couple of months ago, 100 miles it was. That shows I can do it, and I am still as fit as that. You get that way when you ride every day the way I do. Riding fast has helped too to build me up to my present fitness. And I have had to ride fast sometimes! It is a great way of getting away from sticky situations, like dogs chasing you or like when you think you might get run over by a car and you take evasive action. I do not think too many of these new types riding bikes would be able to get out of a tight spot the way I can. They ride too slow and they usually carry too much junk like flags and those big helmets and those jackets they wear. You have to not be carrying much to be really free to move in my opinion.

If upstairs Bill asks where I am, please tell him for me as I will not be leaving him a note. Just between you and me I am sick of his whingeing. He is either bashing my ear, or he wants to play chess all the time. He is too old to play chess anyway, he always forgets the moves he makes. He has just been using me for company lately, I know that. Just like a lot of other people did in the past, except for you however. By the way, I left some stuff in my room like the folding chair and the clock-radio. I burnt all the books and magazines I had as I did not think I would be using them again. You can give the chair and that to anyone who wants it. If I get any mail, which I am not expecting just throw it away if you do not mind. I usually only got junk mail anyway. Everyone always wanting something from you!

I will not have to worry about any of that any more, thank Christ. It will be goodbye Sydney from me. The preparations are done. I got a new chain. I got a couple of spare tyres. I got a new saddle bag (for bikes they are called panniers). I am ready to go.

Probably you will not be hearing from me for a while, Mrs Starkey. I might send you a postcard from somewhere if I feel like it. But do not expect anything. It is only if I feel like it, because that is the way it is going to be from now on. Nothing against you or anything, but everything is going to be different from now on and my bike will see to that. But I have to be honest. Everything is going to be alright to Queensland and then I am not sure. I am going to have to make a decision up there probably. I do not know what I will be doing after Brisbane, maybe that will be the end of the whole thing. Who knows, I might just jump off the bridge up there! ha! ha! I could if I decided to. I am not scared of anything any more.

MY NEIGHBOUR'S DEATH

Being old Fred Leslie's neighbour had never been easy. Over the past three years our relations had soured to such an extent that I had actually come to fear and loathe the man. So much so that in the last few months, I must confess, I had even begun to will his death.

Old Fred died last night. But the joy I had been telling myself would be mine at this event never did transpire. Instead, I spent most of this workday in quiet contemplation; the one interruption being my sole client for the day; the only diversion, a little fantasy on the subject of the old boy's passing.

But that was until a couple of hours ago. This afternoon has brought a revelation, an unexpected late item of news, on the very thing that in the main has occupied my thoughts today. This revelation demands a response from me—and yet its effect has been such that coming to terms with it is proving something of an exercise. Thus, it might be useful to recount what has happened so far.

With only the one person coming in to my shopfront, drop-in welfare agency all day, I had, to repeat, passed the greater part of the time in idle reflection. I had conjectured, for instance, on various aspects of Leslie's exit from this vale of tears: whether he had felt any pain; who, if anyone, had been with him at the time; had the body been discovered some days after his actual demise, or shortly after the fact?

This was a line of thought I had begun last night, when, coming home from a dinner party, I found an ambulance standing at the front of his house. Come to think of it, the sense of peace I have felt most of this day—disturbed though it was a little time ago—also has its roots in the minutes I spent sitting in the car after I got back last night. Those flashing orange lights invariably set one thinking.

Ironically, I had even spent the evening of the dinner party fulminating against the exact same subspecies of human being to which old Fred belonged, the category whose sole preoccupation is money. But as I sat there in my car, parked in the driveway, and watched the ambulancemen wheel the body out on a trolley, I remember thinking what a funny sort of welfare worker I am. There went old Fred, a man who never had any problems with his self-definition, a man who always gave the impression he knew exactly who he was and what he wanted and where he fitted into the scheme of things. And here sat I, who could hardly be said to possess the characteristics supposedly appropriate for someone in the social work and welfare game.

My co-workers, I would have to concede, are more often than not extremely genuine individuals, perhaps erring on the side of earnestness, but nearly always worn down by their struggles on behalf of the needy and oppressed.

While I believe I probably share with them the view that it is a worthwhile occupation to be helping others to help themselves, in the matter of style, there are yawning chasms between us. I have never been the type to sport overalls or jeans, or the sort of serious expression one sees with your average social worker. Or to take another area, against their predilection for alcohol, my favourite drink is nothing more than tea with milk and sugar.

I sometimes think they can never quite believe that someone like me can truly care for people. For my part, when I am depressed, I am certain that the only thing I have in common with the great mass of them is that we are all paid from the same Treasury. Last night, I was convinced that not only did my quirks and fondnesses mark me off from my colleagues, and had led to my being treated with suspicion by them, but that there also just might be something in the popular view that I have a tendency to callousness.

It is curious that I could never seem to bring myself to do anything for Fred Leslie. Chartered accountant though he may have been, why should that have prevented me lending him a hand from time to time with his backyard, or doing some shopping for him, or at least giving him the occasional ear to bend? He was *old*—sixty-five, possibly seventy. As a member of the older generation, he was entitled to a little respect, something which I have always maintained to be a matter of principle.

But today, in the cold light of dawn, so to speak, I realized that was all very well in theory, but in theory alone.

For this particular, now departed individual *did* transgress against me. In fact, he had steadily accumulated a pile of sins against me, and this accounted in no small part for my feelings towards him. Sin as on that sunny day when he saw me working in the front garden of my cottage and came over to warn me against skin cancer and to recommend that I wear a hat in future; sin as in the time his flea-bitten dog took a pull at my trouser leg and he deliberately stood there and did nothing. There were just too many such incidents.

The history of altercations and disputes between us has been extensive and has included at least one very serious blow-up. When I look back on it now, I am tempted to see this event as just a consequence of the old boy's volatile nature, but dead or not, I don't think I can ever forgive him for it.

Until two years ago there was a vacant block of land across the road from us, owned by someone who had long ago left our street to go and live in more salubrious surroundings. Today, the block contains a pair of ghastly two-storey townhouses. I was always opposed to the building of these places; in my demythologizing mode I would explain to anyone who would listen that 'townhouse' was merely a euphemism for 'modern slum terrace'. And when I discovered the notice to build that the developer had placed in the local paper, I was compelled to get up a petition. I canvassed as many people in the street as I could, and the response was heartening. But then came the day Leslie called out to me over the fence and said he wanted to talk to me out in the street.

Suspecting nothing, I went out to the front at his bidding, only to hear him begin an obscene tirade against me. What was the matter with me? he shouted. How dare I object to the developer's plan; there were tens of thousands of people looking for somewhere to live, while I etc. etc. I tried to counter by saying that I certainly wasn't against property, and how dare *he* etc. etc. But then he punched me. He punched me right in the face, and all I could do was run inside to get a handkerchief to staunch the blood running out of my nose.

The memory of the bleeding nose returns to me quite often, only needing the slightest trigger. It came back to me earlier today even, while Mrs Stranieri was sitting opposite me. My only case for the day, she had come in to see me about her husband; could I do something to stop him from continually bashing her? She had made her request in a halting English, and I don't know whether it was that, or the thought of Leslie's assault upon my own self, but at the time I had an odd desire to laugh—I almost lost control. I tricked myself out of it by beginning my rigmarole—counselling her, suggesting a priest, a magistrate's order if that didn't work, and so on. And yet it didn't seem right, that Mrs Stranieri of the five children and brutal husband, could go away crying, and I could sit there with my mind wandering all over the place.

I realize I am finding it increasingly difficult to concentrate while I am at work. Fewer people seem to be coming in these days and so I am left with much idle time. I am in the habit of allowing my imagination to play a little while I am at work anyway, but Fred's passing seemed to provide it with a new stimulus. The non-arrival of my only other listed client for the day, a vexatious litigant by the name of Grahame who had been referred to me by a local solicitor for possible referral elsewhere, allowed me time which I filled by inventing a doleful little fantasy to account for Leslie's death.

Our office on Queen Street, which is the fibro-lined interior of what was once a dry-cleaning shop, is such a dump that looking through the front window at the street outside provides Carol and me with our only relief. (Carol is my assistant two days a week from the Youth Employment Project; her main duties are typing, making me cups of tea, and keeping tabs on the cockroach situation.) What we have you could hardly call a view—there are two desks in the place, and from one of these I gaze out on a dismal and depressed inner-city street, on a dismal and depressed passing parade. The only consolation is the sense of depth and perspective this allows me, the idea that there is something beyond the four walls of my occupation.

My gazing earlier was disturbed by the scurrying of one of our dreaded cockroaches on the floor between my desk and the window. As the warm weather has brought these abominable things out in greater numbers this year, I ordered Carol, who is absolutely fearless with respect to these creatures, to lay some more baits around the room. As I watched her go about this business, kneeling down on the floor in the various corners causing trouble, I returned to the events of last night. The ambulance, the flashing lights, the trolley outside Fred Leslie's house. Only this time, when Fred Leslie was carried out, he was still alive. Alive and kicking. He was being held down on the trolley, but he was trying to break loose. I turned the ambulancemen, those uniformed saviours of life, into two gigantic cockroaches. These cockroaches were dressed in the appropriate garb of blue bomber jackets and navy trousers and jaunty caps; on either side of each one's cap, their antennae stood up tall and free.

The old bastard was as wily and strong as ever, so that at one point he managed to break free of all those dreadful legs pinning him down. But before he could go very far, they had grabbed him again and tripped him into the gutter. Then, looking at each other the two cockroach men quickly formed a pact—it was as if they had silently asked each other what was the point of going on with this charade, what was the point of waiting? They agreed, there was no point. They turned to the prostrate body of the old man and set to work. They began to eat him there and then, in the gutter. They began to tear pieces out of him with those diabolical jaws. The old man's blood began to run, and pretty soon there were only bones and a few pieces of clothing left. Satiated, they put their trolley back in the ambulance, got in it, and drove away ...

Naturally, I should have been ashamed of these thoughts, especially in the light of what I was about to learn. But it *had* been quiet in here and, at that time, there was nothing much else to do. I considered looking at next year's funding proposal forms, but feeling as relaxed as I did, changed my mind in favour of another cup of tea. I was about to ask Carol when, as it happened, I was prevented by the arrival of an unexpected client. I was somewhat annoyed about this at first—Grahame hadn't appeared and here was a person I had never seen before.

The seriousness of what this fellow had to communicate to me soon replaced my agitation at the nuisance I had initially believed him to be. It all started off very badly. He was here, he began, because he felt the Department of Social Security was not giving him his full entitlements. But we weren't two minutes into the interview when he decided to question my bona fides. I didn't look like a welfare worker, he said, among other things. My retort to this was that it was foolish to presume that someone who wore a collar and tie was to be automatically counted as an enemy. His T-shirt and tattered jeans didn't bother me, why should my apparel cause him any concern? I also told him that I was being paid by the Government, and the Government had careful selection procedures when it came to employing people whose job was ultimately to help those in need.

After further clarifications along these lines, I thought I had him finally straightened out when he broke down and began to cry. Through the tears, he managed to get out that he had something else he wanted to say—the missing entitlements were only part of his problems. Nothing unusual about this, I told myself;

they often play this little game where they come on a pretext, eventually breaking down to reveal that there is something far more serious than a missed cheque concerning them. In this instance, I have to confess, the revelation was to some extent unnerving.

It came out that by last night he was down to his last dollar or two, this character, and had talked himself into doing a break and enter, with the idea he might be able to lift something for which he could get some cash. He had gone to Clyde Street—Clyde Street, in Petersham, my own street that is—and picked out a darkened house. He jumped the back fence and entered through the un-locked back door. There, in the laundry, a light suddenly came on, and he was confronted by an old man.

My mind raced ahead of him here—I knew whose house he was talking about; I knew to whom he was refer-ring. I began steeling myself to hear the grim account of a bashing or murder—not the first one I might add, but they are never easy—the gory details of Fred Leslie's demise.

That, I was fortunately spared; he said that he never touched the old man—he kept repeating that he nev-er touched him—but that all of a sudden the old boy standing not two metres in front of him just keeled over. He bent over to see what had happened, but realized he was touching a dead man, a corpse. This threw him into such a panic that he jumped up and 'ran like blazes', as he put it, to get away from there.

He was here, he said, because he felt guilty. He just knew he was responsible for what had happened. He wanted to know what he should do next. Should he give himself up to the cops, or what? He needed advice.

I told him, first off, that it was always dangerous telling someone you don't know a story of the kind he had just related. A priest might be bound to stay mum, but there weren't too many other people in authority whom one could count on. I was obliged, after what I had just been told, to get on the phone to the police and tell them what I knew.

In the silence that followed I thought to myself how useful it was that the other fellow, Grahame, hadn't turned up. But I was, at that stage, genuinely in need of a cup of tea. I asked 'Mr Smith'—I called him that in the interests of maintaining anonymity—whether he wanted a cup himself, but he declined. On my way to put the jug on, I told little Carol she could go home—although I was certain she hadn't heard anything, her presence was a complicating factor.

I locked the front door after her and went back to the spare room where I poured the water into my mug and added a teabag and waited. Once more today, I felt like laughing—a very strong need to let go seemed to be manifesting itself. Oddly enough, I often feel this urge when I am in an unassailable position, when I have the upper hand in some situation or other. The knowledge that I had quickly to come up with a gambit on the matter of this unsolicited confession to which I had been privy, soon brought me back to my senses.

In the main office again, which is where I sit at this

moment, the young lout continued to occupy the chair in front of my desk, with the same desperate and dejected air about him. A closer look at his face indicated that he was about eighteen or nineteen, making him most susceptible, I considered, to what I had in mind.

'Well Mr Smith, and no, don't tell me your right name ... there is no doubt you have committed a crime ...' He looked up at me then with a defeated and expectant expression, waiting for I don't know what, perhaps for me to tell him I was going to call the police. 'But yours has been a petty crime—a break and enter. In the final analysis you are not responsible—it seems to me—for the death of that old man. Who knows what was wrong with him? There is every likelihood he had some condition which was going to kill him anyway ... Now you've told me this story of yours, and I do believe you have been telling the truth. You can rest assured, you can bank on it, that it will stay here with me ... I won't be telling anyone, I promise you. You have my word ...'

At this, it looked as if he was about to start crying again. I put a stop to the chance of that happening by coming around to his side of the desk and placing my hand on his shoulder. His face began to relax; in a while he looked nothing but tremendously relieved. I then ran through the routine about where he could go to sort out his social security problem and explained to him that the best thing he could do now was to leave.

As I led him to the door, I looked at my watch—it was just before five, an hour ago—and told him that I didn't ever want to see him again. He nodded without looking at me and went out into the street. And I went back to my desk to finish my tea ... I have been sitting here ever since, the empty cup on a manila folder in front of me. In short, I have been ruminating.

I am in the habit of setting time aside each afternoon to make an interpretation of the day's phenomena. I find a summing-up is very useful, for if and when I am able to establish some meaning or pattern, I am heartened, and can think of tomorrow as a clean slate. But here on my own, as this day winds down, I have had some difficulty in trying to make sense of everything—it has all been quite out of the ordinary.

Looking back, there is no doubt I have probably done something to help that young fool expiate his feelings of guilt. I understand also that measured against the evil that is abroad, my own culpability in the isolated incident of my neighbour's death is practically negligible. If an obituary were in order, one could certainly speak of the life and death of Fred Leslie in Christian terms, and extract a higher meaning; my own faults, these also could be judged as an all too typical example of the Fall from Grace—if one were a Christian, that is.

But something else begins to suggest itself. My thoughts have at last found their words and, as is my usual practice, I will put them on paper. I take my pad and my pen and I write—

'Events have reaffirmed my belief that there *are* those days, rare and precious days, when human affairs indeed look to have their beginnings and ends, when life *does* present us with the occasional denouement. We observe an entrance, we observe an exit; we see that exit to be a perfect function of the particular modality of a particular life. And all through, our observation is accompanied by a sense of the very rightness of all that has happened. We have all played a part in Mr Leslie's life, even the unexpected "Mr Smith". Indeed, "Mr Smith" could be said to have served a very special purpose in the cycle of the subject's life. About that young idiot, there is nothing more I can say or do. Have I not told him, more or less, that as far as I am concerned, he no longer exists? And as for people in the welfare game, while human misery continues to multiply, there will always be something for us to be going on with.'

VELODROME

It was heading towards five o'clock and he had missed part of the programme. A bit late, but never mind, there would still be plenty of good racing. He dug in his pocket for the three dollars, handed it to the woman at the entrance, and passed through the turnstile.

Finding a spot was the next question. The place was pretty full; the stand was crowded, and there was a lot of confusion around the gate opening on to the centre of the track where all the riders and their bikes were marshalled. There was no other choice but a position somewhere near the guard rail. From there, he could look down at the riders as they whizzed past.

He walked right round the edge of the track to where he found a gap among the people lining the rail. He spread his hands wide to take hold of the steel tube, and then leaned his weight against it. According to the announcer, there would be a delay before the next race—a junior handicap—was ready to go. The officials were still trying to get a full list of riders together.

He looked up at the sky. Clear now, but with Sydney summer afternoons, you never knew. It could always come down when you least expected it. The track had no roof and, being up here on this hill, was very exposed.

Wasn't there a better place to put it? He could never work out why they put it here where it could only catch all the wind. One good thing about being on a hill though, you could see the thunderstorms coming no trouble at all.

It was getting on for dusk. Twilight. The clouds over Botany Bay were streaked with purple, there was a weird light over the airport in the distance. From here, you could look down on the airport a couple of kilometres away—the planes coming down, going away, the lights, the radar tracking round and round, looking and looking.

A tap on his back, and then someone came up next to him. It was Teddy.

'Ray, old son! How are you?'

'Not bad Ted, not bad, how about you?'

'Actually, I'm a wreck, but I don't like goin' on about it. Know what I mean?'

Ted was always hard to follow, the way he was so quick. He never felt comfortable around blokes like him—they were always sending you up. But when they had both turned away from each other to face the track again, he did think of something to say to him.

'It's like a saucer really, like the radar dish over there.'

'What is?'

'This velodrome. The way it's turned up around the edge. I mean, you can see the likeness, can't you?'

He was conscious then of Ted looking at him sideways for a bit of a while—which made him feel uncomfortable. Then he heard him say—

'Listen Ray, gotta go. Son's racing this afternoon, and I've got to go out in the middle to check his bike. Kid would forget his head if it wasn't screwed on!'

Ted was gone before he could say anything back to him. Not that he felt put out or anything. He was happy to have been saved the trouble.

On the other side of the track, where the grandstand was, people were shifting about, getting themselves ready for the next race. Those who had cushions were moving them around on the concrete seats, trying to prevent the sore arse you got when you sat in the stand. Now the bloke with the hot dogs was starting up, fool that he was. The same bloke every week, yelling 'Doggies! Doggies! Doggies!' while everyone was trying to concentrate on the races. Some kids in the stand were making fun of him; they were calling out 'Doggies!' too.

The kids who were about to race in the handicap had started doing their warm-up laps. With delays like this it was going to be a long night by the time it was all over. He looked at his programme again. Later, the Aces would be riding a One-Hour Madison, and that would be worth watching. The last race he himself had ridden was a Madison, three years ago. Hard to ride, but good to watch. It would be good to be still young enough to start up in something like this, but you couldn't stay a kid forever.

In the centre of the track, those who weren't doing warm-up laps were sitting around, some on the grass, some on fold-up chairs. The sensible ones had rugs over their legs. With that wind, you had to keep them warm, summer or no summer. It was getting darker, and the northeaster off the bay was starting to get stronger. The only plus was there were no clouds.

He spotted a couple of familiar faces out there in the middle. Chris King and Tony Sutherland. In the programme it said they would be lining up for the Madison too. They were kidding themselves, both of them were around his age, at least forty-five. You can only push yourself so far.

The early races had been boring, the youngsters weren't quick enough to make it interesting. They were nervous at the start and they jumped the gun every time. Restart. Restart again. The problem was with their dads, the way they held them at the line. Hand on the saddle, hand on the bars, all they had to do was let go of them at the gun; but no, they kept giving them these helpful little shoves— and that was cheating. He was glad, in a way, that he never had an old man to give him that sort of trouble.

Now, just before the start of the Madison, he occupied himself looking out over the rooftops, toward the airport and the bay. In his mind's eye, he marked out the expressway, snaking its way towards Kingsford Smith, from that line of orange-coloured lamps. A bright orange, they were; against the ink blue of the sky as it was at the moment, they made a pretty spectacular combination. It occurred to him, also, those colours made a Broadmeadow Club jumper.

The track lights suddenly came on and those colours were lost. The concrete circle turned white. The two straights, the two bends, the whole three hundred metres, all white. A Ribbon of Light—the same sort of thing as they had at the Night Trots, a Ribbon of Light. He was trying to remember the last time he had been to the trots when the bloke in the booth announced that the Madison was about to begin.

'I think we're ready ladies and gentlemen ... This one is for two-man teams—a series of sprints for points and money. One rider goes for broke in the sprint each five laps, his partner takes it easy, then they swap over.'

He counted the number of teams on the programme. Ten, including Chris and Tony. A hundred and fifty dollars for the team with the most sprint points at the end—ten dollars per sprint along the way.

'There's the gun and, oh mate, is there anything like the Madison for go and excitement?'

Two young Blacktown riders began pouring it on.

'They're hoping to get a break on the field, folks. Pick up the sprint points with no competition. Very cunning ... But the others are starting to peg them back ... Never that easy, is it folks?'

He heard a part of the crowd in the grandstand yell 'Noooo!! ...'

Just after halfway, and old Chris was obviously finding the going hard. He watched as Tony did the next three sprints himself to let his partner get his breath back. It didn't seem to make much difference—they were both starting to drop back ...

Getting towards the end, they were running fifth on points. Way down compared to the leading team. They still had an outside chance, but they weren't getting anywhere. He focused on the lap board and began to concentrate. There were only three sprints to go, but for the old mates, a win or place was looking to be out of the question. They were still rolling around, almost as if for form's sake, he supposed so they could say they finished.

But then he saw it—a way back up for the two veterans in the field. He added up the numbers again; if they could win the final three sprints, they could still come out on top. And there was a way.

It was a matter of Tony, Tony who looked to be going the better of the two, sticking close to number eight's back wheel. He had been leading a lot of the sprint winners into the home straight, that one; he didn't have a strong enough kick to win them himself, but he was worth following for the slipstream. If Tony could stay behind him and then come around him in the straight, there was every chance of picking up some more points. It wasn't impossible. The hard part, he saw as he looked at the crowd around the gate, was going to be in finding a way to call that idea out to them.

The noise was too loud for him to try and shout across the guard rail. Besides, the speed they were going past, there was no way either of them would be able to hear him. He would have to get down into the inside of the track, where it was quieter, and he could get close enough to them for them to get the message. If he could get inside, he could wave to get their attention.

He pushed his way out through the people massed at his back and walked quickly to the gate further around. A bloke in a dust coat stood guard; he had a red flag to wave at anyone who tried to get across while the riders were approaching.

'Hey mate,' he called out to him, 'I've gotta get into the middle.'

'Not now you can't. Race is nearly over.'

By the look on this bloke's face, it was obvious he wasn't going to make any exceptions.

'But I've got a message for a couple of the riders.'

'I said you can't get across.'

To make it even harder, this official-type then pushed his fat body against the gate, so that he couldn't slip across while he wasn't looking. That was that. He stood there feeling frustrated, helplessly watching proceedings come to an end. No one gave you a chance; even when you had a few answers, no one ever gave you a chance.

The kid from Blacktown and his little mate went on to win it—all of eighteen years old they were, by the look of them. Sixty-three points to King's and Sutherland's forty-seven.

Soon after, things began to wind up. He didn't want to get caught in the crush of people leaving and so went and sat on an empty seat in the bottom of the stand. From there, he watched them all filing out. At one point, he looked back and up at the rows of seats climbing away behind him. At the top of the stand, in a little booth up there, he saw the announcer switch off the PA and pack up his gear, getting ready to leave.

It was taking a while, but then he was in no hurry to go anywhere. He was happy to sit there and feel the breeze against his skin, so refreshing on a humid night like this. He watched the scraps of paper and empty chip packets blowing down the steps, swirling around on the track itself, like it was time for them to go too.

The last rider carried his machine on his shoulder out of the marshalling area. And following him, the slob with the flag went as well. Just looking at him walking into the tunnel under the stand made him angry; he imagined himself leaning across and putting an axe through his head.

Then, the lights went off. No one seemed to have noticed he was still there.

He would stay a bit longer. On a night like this, the breeze did nothing for the falling-down dump at Erskineville where he lived; it was locked in on all sides, a real oven. He could think of better places to spend a hot night. For instance, what was there to stop him staying right here? He could stay here no trouble at all. He could sleep right here under this grandstand, say, where it was sure to be cool.

The noise of the cars starting up and leaving the parking lot was coming to an end. It was all quiet at last. The only sound came from the rubbish, moved by the wind, scratching along the concrete. He sat there in the stillness for a few more minutes.

He was starting to feel a bit cold, and with that, knew he really couldn't stay here tonight. When all was said and done, you could never just do whatever you felt like doing. If he stayed here, who was to say he wouldn't be bailed up by a security man, or a cop? All sorts of things probably went on here at night.

He got up to go, and, turning into the aisle, again saw the announcer's booth. It had no door, it was just a plywood box with a sort of canvas awning and open on both sides. He was curious about it, and thought he might have a look inside before he left. He climbed the aisle stairs, the half-dozen rows to the top.

It seemed strange that it was open like this. But then they probably didn't count on anyone being left behind like him; they did lock the outer gates at the end of each carnival.

He sat in the chair. The announcer's microphone was directly in front, screwed down onto a small table. He couldn't see any other gear in the booth itself, no knobs or switches of the sort you might expect. But as he moved his feet around under the table, he felt something there. He looked down and there it was, the amplifier or whatever it was called.

He put his hands around the microphone. It was like being in charge of something up here. The view over everything was perfect, he was beginning to get a good idea of what it would be like to call the races from this spot. It wouldn't be all that hard.

No, not very hard at all. He leaned over again and

ran his fingers over the front of the amplifier, trying the various switches. One of them eventually brought on a little red light. He tapped the microphone—there was power alright.

'Ladies and gentlemen,' that's how the other bloke began—'Ladies and gentlemen ...' it was funny saying that. He heard his voice carry out and around the velodrome and then return to him. A very strange feeling, it was. It made his fingers tingle. What would happen if he went on? The velodrome was out of the way up here; he was pretty sure nobody would hear anything.

And he sure as onions knew what he wanted to say next.

'Yes, looks like King and Sutherland are coming back up through the field. King's got the right idea. He's sticking to that young bloke's back wheel like Tarzan's Grip. Here he comes ... Yes! A sprint win to King! ...'

He reran the race for himself in the darkness. Then, a few laps later—

'There's still life in those old-timers folks! King's done it again! Another sprint win ... They've got it sewn up ... Yes, there it is, a win to the veterans in the field ...'

Just as he finished, he had this panicky idea that he should get up and run away. He got out of the chair and went down on his knees to switch the thing off. But in those moments of fumbling around under the table, the silence became obvious again. What was there to be afraid of? There was simply no-one around.

He straightened up, and sat back on the chair.

Bugger it, there was something else he wanted to do; that is, something else he wanted to say.

He leaned forward and put his mouth close to the microphone. He started softly; with a mike all you had to do was whisper, and it did the rest.

'Ladies and gentlemen ... we've got something special for youse now. An old cyclist from yesteryear—I'm sure you all remember him—Ray Lambert. Yes, that's right, give him a hand. Well Ray is with us here tonight. We thought you'd like to see the old champ do a lap of honour—and he's obliged us ... Go on Ray, off you go ...'

And he saw himself do that three hundred-metre circuit, just like the old days, say after he had won his specialty, the ten-mile scratch race. One hand on the handlebars, the other free and waving to the spectators, or maybe holding a victory bouquet ...

For someone who knew himself to be not much of a talker, he was tickled at the way the words were coming out, the funny sort of confidence that had come over him. He understood he had been waiting a long time for a chance like this. He realized too there were lots more things he felt like saying.

'A couple of other things—before I get off. To the chap at the gate who wouldn't let me through—you're a bloody slug, mate. And a drongo ... And as for that dirty bastard mongrel who took my wallet last week—if I ever get my hands on you, I'll shoot you ... To all the shit-heads who've given me a hard time over the years—you can All Go And Get Fucked!!'

A noise. He thought he heard a noise in the parking lot, a door slammed shut or something. Maybe the place wasn't empty at all, and he had been found out. He ducked down quickly to switch off the PA. Just being on made it give off a low hum.

He waited without moving. The minutes passed and he heard nothing more. He was coming round to thinking the noise hadn't been in the car park, but probably somewhere up the street. Whatever, it was a dangerous game he was playing here, there was no guarantee he hadn't been heard.

And at last there was nothing left but to go—not that he wanted to get going. He had to admit to himself that he was a bit scared of staying here the rest of the night; he was just too much of a coward.

He looked out from the booth for the last time, out over the track, to the airport beyond. Such a terrific view from up here, you felt so on top of things.

There was the radar, still doing its job. He wondered if it was picking him up. Now there was a thought—was it capable of picking him up? He was high enough wasn't he? What do they actually look for, those things? Was it an electrical signal, or something more? If an aeroplane was just a shape in the dark, giving off a signal, what was he?

BILLY AND THE BIRDS

'Billy reckons there's fewer gannets this year than ever before.'

Mrs Billy Fletcher turned from the tea-making to tell June this. She waited for a sign from her friend, and when it came—a nod—she turned to take the water off the stove, then poured it into the pot.

She carried the teapot to the table and sat herself down. But she had forgotten the cups, and so put her palms on the table and pushed herself up again. Her friend waved her down.

'I know where they are, sit down. I know where they are.'

Mrs Billy sat down obediently and let June go to the cupboard.

'Don't bother about matched,' Mrs Billy called to her.

'No, alright.'

June returned with odd cups and saucers. She set them on the table and was about to reach for milk and the sugar bowl when Mrs Billy beat her to them. She went on to put the customary milk and sugar in each.

'They're getting to be fewer each year, you know.'

'Is that so? How does he know?'

'The banding.'

'Oh, that's right. He puts those rings on them, doesn't he.'

'Not on his own but, June. He's got other people helping him, you know. Phil from the Depot and young Ross, the one from Mead and Thorpe's. They're always giving him a hand.'

'Yes, that's right. I know that.'

June liked to reassure her friend. She always did her best to help Mrs Billy buck up. If you had a husband as silly as hers she supposed you'd have to feel a bit low from time to time. Him and his birds. It made her feel a little cross.

He wasn't the only bloke around here who you could call a bit quirky—she could think of one or two other Peninsula boys who had funny ideas. But none of them had Billy's mania for birds. He'd been at it like a religion for at least thirty years as far as she could recall. Everyone knew him as the 'local authority'.

'But where would he be now Mrs B.? Would you know that?'

'He's down at the coast, June. He always tells me where he's going.'

'I'm not suggesting anything, love.'

Billy was out on the Peninsula coast, opposite the stack known as Pulpit Rock. He had his binoculars trained on the stack, a seasonal home to the local breed of gannets. For generations, tens of thousands of them had come to this offshore rock each year to burrow and nest, but in recent times their numbers had dropped off. Billy felt it his duty to keep track of them.

It was late in the season, most of the birds had moved on, but it was important to know how many stragglers were left behind. There were always a few left behind.

As it was getting on towards five, the light was too poor for him to be staying on much longer. He took up the case and packed the Zeiss glasses away, then placed it carefully on the ledge next to him. He liked doing that, putting the binoculars in their leather case—they fitted so snugly. They were a good pair, powerful, and sturdy enough to take a knock.

His legs were stiff from crouching, and so he stood for a time gazing out over the ocean before beginning the walk back up the track. This afternoon he had seen six pairs altogether. A sizeable number really. He felt for his notepad in his back pocket, but remembered he had left it in the ute. He would put the numbers in later. He set off slowly to climb the slope, the hundred metres or so back to the top.

He didn't much feel like going home. The possibility of calling into town and having a chat to young Ross down at Mead's crossed his mind. Since last year when he'd come to live in this area, and joined the Society, Billy had slowly taken to him. He was becoming known as Billy's 'offsider'. But as for seeing him today, it was getting a bit late, the store would be closed by the time he got into town.

Besides, she'd only go off. She'd been going off more and more of late, and he had no taste for another blue. It wasn't easy putting up with her antics anymore. A while back, he had been thinking of getting rid of her. But there was the farm—his wife and the farm, they were his lot really, for better or for worse.

Back at the ute, it was definitely too dark to go to town. He took instead the familiar road back, back into the dairy country, and the place he had always called his 'old patch'. He had talked to Ross more than once about his feelings for the place—with Ross you could do that because although he worked in a store in town, he too was from farming stock.

Billy liked the way this young fellow talked about the land; he had a sort of respect for it. Which was more than you could say for Mrs Billy, who had grown up in Leongatha. She had never really been keen on moving to the farm after they got married. Not really. She had never even tried to like it, or so it seemed to him, and he'd given up trying to make her see reason a long, long time ago.

June twisted her saucer slowly, and every now and then would look at Mrs Billy. But there was not much value in her today. For June, it was a matter of knowing how to handle a bloke like Billy Fletcher. There was a knack to it. For a start, you didn't let them get away with too much. When he started up about the birds around these parts being 'his', for instance, and that sort of thing, you would just tell him to pull his head in. And if he didn't, well he could go to buggery.

'Would you like some more tea June?' Mrs B. asked her quietly.

'No thanks, love ... It's getting on a bit. By the way, isn't it time the pioneer was getting home?'

Mrs B. looked up at her friend and wondered why she had spoken like that.

'Won't be long now probably ...'

It was hard to get Mrs B. to bite on this subject. This business about her husband being a descendant of the original settlers around here. Everyone agreed, like shy Phil at the Depot, that the Fletchers had been here first, but no-one knew the details. Although not really expecting him to know much, she had even pressed young Ross about it one time when she had gone in to buy a new kerosene heater.

She had come up to him at his counter in the hardware part, and got talking. But she couldn't get the devious little so and so to say much about old Billy. Like his mate, all he wanted to talk about were the birds.

'Don't know about that Mrs. He loves the birds though, and I'm helpin' him so as we can save 'em. They're disappearin' fast.'

'Oh yes,' she had asked, 'and why would that be, do you reckon?'

'It's the pollution in the atmosphere that's killin' 'em off. We can tell from the bandin' what's happenin' with different species—that's why we do it, the bandin' I mean.'

'But how would that help—I don't know much about birds, but I can't see how that's going to help, can you?'

He never answered the question. The little runt got all tight-lipped instead, pretending he was too busy to talk any longer. He was certainly learning his mate's bad habits fast—like not being able to answer a straight question. The men around these parts, they were all like that; they were all, as far as she could make out, off their rockers.

By the time Billy got home, June was gone. His wife was at the sink, washing up. A good sign he was late for tea.

'It's in the oven. There's foil on it. You can heat it up if you want it.'

As she had spoken without turning from the sink, he had an idea he was in the bad books. He took the lighter, got down on his haunches, and lit the stove himself.

'What temperature?'

No answer.

'Ay? What temperature should I put it on?'

'Three-fifty.'

This she said again without turning, and more sharply, and he knew it was on again. Not that he ever let this sort of carry-on of hers ever rattle him. He sat at the table to wait, then remembered he still hadn't recorded the gannet numbers.

He got up quietly and went outside to retrieve the pad from the ute. He had found the pad and was about to close the door when he heard something odd. A cockatoo screeching. A gang-gang at that. The squawking and carry-on that the birds made around here at dusk was well and truly over. But this lone bird was still at it, somewhere out in the yard near the machinery shed. Maybe in the candle bark next to it. He went down to investigate.

He made his way there slowly and stood quietly for a minute or two, trying to home in on the sound. It was too dark to see much. The bird was making quite a racket, but in amongst it he heard the back door of the house open. He turned to see his wife appear in silhouette in the doorway.

'You haven't forgotten the food again, have you?'

'No I haven't, as a matter of fact,' he called back to her. 'I was on me way.'

Back inside, he went to the oven and took the plate of food out. He didn't use a glove, and by the time he was at the table he was juggling it in his hands, so hot had it become. He removed the foil and the baked chicken and vegetables were steaming, too hot to eat. He pushed the plate to one side, and took out the pad instead. He began to write, slowly, with great care, the details of what he had seen this afternoon.

From where she stood at the sink, wiping up, Mrs Billy became aware of the silence at the table. She looked over her shoulder and saw he wasn't eating.

'For God's ... you're letting it get cold again.'

'I've got to write down what I've got to write down, alright?'

His wife felt she wanted to say something, but nothing more would come. She never could argue with him the way he could argue with her. She turned back to the dishes, face reddened, sweat trickling down her temples.

She tried to make the rest of the wiping up as noisy as she could. The cutlery she practically threw into the plastic container.

Billy pushed the food away and went to his room— they had long since gone their separate ways over sleeping arrangements. It suited Billy. Since he had taken over the spare bedroom, he had more room for his bird books and his photographic and other equipment.

He went straight for the folder. He took it down from a shelf—a big black ring-folder. Opened flat at any point, it contained a photo of a bird on the left hand page, in a plastic cover, and on the right a page of typed information relating to that bird. Whenever he was agitated, or Mrs Billy had been playing up, and it was night, he would go to his room, take down this folder and leaf through it.

He was building a catalogue of the birds of the Peninsula, his Peninsula. He had been working at it for years now, and was getting pretty well near the end. In an area he had originally marked off on an old land grant map given to him by his father, he had—with the assistance of some other local birdwatchers—managed to find one hundred and thirty-seven different species. He had, however, made no new discoveries for the last thirteen or fourteen months.

He was still on the lookout though. If there was spare time during the day, he filled it by going out in the ute to one of his favourite watching spots. Even if he had long ago accounted for the birds at any particular place, he still liked to go out.

Being one of the originals hereabouts, he felt an obligation to the local wildlife. His wife had never been able to understand that; couldn't get it into her thick head. He'd made concessions. Again, something Mrs Billy hadn't ever acknowledged. Some work, nest checking for instance, or the owls, you had to do at night. But because she'd only go off, he had always stayed at home during the evenings. He was the restless type, he liked to keep busy, and he didn't like having to stay indoors when he could be out working on the birds.

He got to the gannet photos, ones he'd taken years ago. A familiar angle; he had taken these from the location he had visited earlier today.

Jeezus. A thumping in his chest began. JEEZUS—he said it out aloud this time. He'd left his glasses out there. He knew he had. He glanced around the room for form's sake, but he was sure, and he was up on his feet and on his way out.

She was still in the kitchen when he went there to get his keys. She was sitting at the table with her head in her hands. He spoke to her heading for the door.

'I gotta go out.'

Mrs Billy looked up, disbelieving. But by this time he was half outside. She wanted to say something, to say something to get him back inside. But like always, it never came when she wanted it. Nothing came, but a feeling of dizziness and nausea.

Billy was almost at the ute when he heard her. First a moaning noise. And then she was screaming, making an awful sound, like a fire engine siren, she was going loud and soft, up and down. He'd never heard her make that noise before.

He considered it to be blackmail.

Opening the door of the car, he heard a new noise, once more from inside the house. From what he could tell, his wife was now thumping the kitchen table, as if it were a bloody drum or something.

He put his seatbelt on and started the engine.

If she was going to carry on like that, she could go to buggery. He had more important things on his mind at the moment. Those glasses had cost twelve hundred dollars. But apart from that, without them, there was no way he could finish the job he'd set out to do.

Other blokes went out every night of the week, getting up to all sorts of tricks. And drinking too. He'd been faithful all his life. If she couldn't see that, then bad luck for her.

June was making the tea. A week since the funeral, and old Mrs B. was only beginning to be able to talk again. She was still needing a helping hand, and to her neighbour it seemed only right.

She hadn't asked which cups today. But Mrs Billy did notice that she had brought matched to the table. 'You didn't have to June.'

'No trouble really.'

June took this as a sign. That she had noticed such a thing at all meant she must be on the improve. And why not? Why anyone would waste time mourning a nut like Billy Fletcher was beyond her. It had been his own stupid fault anyway—going out in the middle of the night and falling off a cliff.

'You're looking a bit better, Mrs Billy.'

The new-made widow looked at her friend and managed to bring on a tired smile. She had an idea she should be thanking her friend for her help with everything over the past ten days. But then that could wait.

'He wanted to do the right thing by the birds, the native birds.'

'Yes, I know that Mrs B.'

'Funny, he used to say he was a native, just like some of them ... His people first settled this district, you know ...'

'Yes, I'd heard, Mrs B ... Look, I don't know about this ... I know you never minded being called what you're called, but after what's happened ... maybe I should call you ... you know.'

'Moira? No, don't call me that, I don't like Moira. I'm still Mrs Billy, June. I always will be.'

ISLANDS

All this has come about because of my wanting to be useful, wanting to play my part. The Committee made me the offer, and I responded. The Committee said I could help us put it all together. I sincerely believe it was their fault that I fell from grace.

We want to know about Our Heritage, they said. Can you help? Sure, fine, I said. No problems. Just tell me what you want to know about, give me some money, and send me out. I'll come back with the goods.

Islands, for instance. We discover that we are surrounded by Islands. Should we not consider them? Aren't they part of the picture too? Of course they are. We ought to know about all our Islands—from A to Z.

I was told that X and Y had never been done. I'll do them, I said. Just give me the money and no worries—I'll have the info in no time at all.

In the above I am describing the behaviour of a well-meaning but at the same time corrupt fool. This fool, me, has become the world's foremost authority on these Islands. Bearing in mind I have in my time studied many Islands, X and Y are the ones I have covered in the greatest detail.

Why? Because they asked me to do it. This was at a

time when I thought it was impossible to refuse a sacred task. In those days I could never be accused of not doing my bit for the New Society.

I turn now to address you, the individuals on the committee, the men who sent me to these places, to Islands X and Y. Please try to listen. To you I have this to say—

Thanks a lot, pals.

You've given me some terrible nightmares.

Not for the prosy reasons you might be contemplating—like the actual work of getting to these places and gathering the material. That was nothing. That was no trouble at all. I'm talking about the real nightmares, the ones I've had ever since I first visited, you guessed it, Islands X and Y.

The nightmares started after I got back home from these places. Which was after I had discovered they had offshore Islands of their own. *They* are what continue to fill my dreams at night. *They* are the real problem.

As you well know, Island X is in the Pacific, and Island Y is in the Mediterranean. We agreed before I set out on these capers a decade ago, that they were both significant because they were both, in different ways, part of Our Experience. Our first settlers colonized X in the early days, but then forgot about the place, more or less left it to its own devices. On the other hand, many of our later settlers came from Y after the War. In the intervening period, Y has also been forgotten.

They were really easy to do, you know. Camera, notepads, a few interviews with the locals, an amount of research in libraries and so on, and hey presto! We are ready to go into print! The books will remind everyone, will make them think about Who We Are, will make them all aware of their cultural traditions. That's what you said to me.

But what you didn't know, indeed nobody here knew, was that Island X had its own tiny little rocky outcrop a few hundred metres off its northern coast—in other words its own Island! I have since named this one Island X(i). And Island Y, the same thing, a little island further out—only in this case off the southern tip. This one I call Island Y(i).

These are the places I have been trying to forget. All the years since I 'did' them, they have been plaguing me. I wish I could go back to the days before I ever knew they existed. I think I was probably happier then.

I hope you anonymous gentlemen are paying attention. There is nothing difficult about what I am saying. This isn't fiction. I don't write fiction, as you above all must be aware. This is not some story, trading off 'mysteries' and 'enigmas', busily developing the felicitous ambiguities one sees in certain kinds of literary prose. I will lay it all out for you, you bastards, plain and simple. So that (a) you can see what you've done to me, and (b) you might finally understand something about the nature of knowledge about ourselves, and (c) as a result, leave me alone.

I must tell you, by the way, that in the critical phase of this last psychic upheaval I had an idea that if I sat down and wrote out all the details about these extra Islands, these unexpected accessories to X and Y, I might be able to purge myself.

I never got around to doing that because I realized there was no point. All was permanently etched in my brain anyway, like you might brand a piece of leather. I really have no need to write anything down about these places, these rocks which have become such features in the geography of my dreams. If you'd like to know, I can reel it all off by heart anyway.

But at one stage I did stupidly think that fully detailed, then fully analysed, these places might just disappear, and be replaced by sleep, sleep of the kind I haven't had for years. It hasn't proved possible.

I do have a full tape of the analysis in my head, if you are curious. In fact I think I will tell you whether you are or you aren't.

We can pass over X and Y themselves very briefly, for they are clichés. Y is a typical impoverished Mediterranean island of the sort which has been sending us its children for decades. This place is really part of a foreign country where the system of inheritance puts such pressure on land, the plots then become too small to support anybody, and emigration follows. X was a place we used to help with our social hygiene—this was where we once upon a time sent all those people who broke Our Laws, who never seemed to be able to fit in happily.

Anyway, you've got all this—I delivered it all up to you when you wanted it, didn't I?

No, let's get to the guts of it.

Island X(i)?

This is a volcanic remnant, two kilometres from X, and itself about two kilometres wide. Unlike the main Island, it has no history of human habitation. You can see it from X; it rises sheer from the water and is quite high. It is apparently barren—although no one knows why that is so. It is also spectacular to look at. From X it looks like a series of slashes of colour; the rock formations are in red, purple, crimson, yellow, orange. Perhaps this is what the planet Mars looks like.

I wanted to get over to see that Island from up close, but I never made it. Why? Because no one would help me. I asked the natives whether there was a boat. No, they said. There is no reason to go there. Nobody goes there, nobody has ever been there. There's nothing to see ... that's what the ones who were willing to talk at all said—the others just shrugged or shook their heads. There was an awful lot of shrugging and head-shaking on X, I'll tell you.

In the dream I am standing inside the collapsed walls of the old gaol by the sea. I am not really imprisoned— in real life I walked in, in real life I walked out—but I am standing there holding some kind of plant and looking across the water to X(i) and crying because I want to get over there, I want to be there but I can't. I desperately want to be there, but there is no way. Not only because there are no boats, but because I can't move. I am immobilized. My legs refuse to take me anywhere, no matter how hard I try to get them moving.

Over and over again, I have this blasted dream.

It alternates with the Island Y(i) dream.

Island Y(i)?

This is a small outcrop of limestone in the sea less than five hundred metres from the main coastal town of Y. Unlike at X, the locals here had at least a few things to tell me about this outcrop. It had never had a name, as far as anyone could tell, but the man who ran the cafe told me that in the sixteenth century it was a marine fortress belonging to one or other of the maritime Dukes of Venice. What looked like the remains of an old fort could still be distinguished from Y.

What was left of this structure, they told me, was used a hundred years ago as a shelter for lepers, and an infirmary. They didn't know how much of this usage could still be seen as no-one had been across since it closed down over fifty years ago.

It was late afternoon of a winter's day ten years ago when I went down to the port and hired a caique powered by a small petrol engine. Here I would not be thwarted.

The boat was moored at a little wooden wharf. Walking along that wharf I looked down and saw an ancient, submerged pier running right alongside. I stood and stared down through the clear water lapping over the top of it. It was still more or less intact and seemed to be made of marble blocks. I remember wondering why storms or tides had never washed it all away.

The stretch of water between Y and Y(i) was so quiet, one couldn't but believe it had always been like this, and always would be. I set off across an oil-flat calm, with the sound of the two-stroke engine for company.

The dream always starts with this vivid component of going across the water. I have to tell you, however, in some versions I wade across by walking along the old pier.

The next bit is always the same as it was in reality.

I run the boat up a shingle beach where I tie it up by throwing a rope around a large rock. I walk over the beach and get to an old track which seems to lead up to the ruins, and does so. Once at the top, I walk onto what looks like a parade ground with the object of getting to what's left of an old archway or entrance on the far side. Centuries ago, this was probably used as a place for assembling the soldiery. But now it was paved with concrete, concrete which couldn't have been more than seventy or eighty years old, and marked out in little squares, about a metre by a metre.

I walk across this ground where, at one point, in the middle of one of these small squares, the concrete gives way. There is a crack and my leg goes through and down into a hole as far as my knee. I pull up one of the bits of broken concrete to free my leg. I get it out again, then get on my hands and knees to look down. A cranium and arm and leg bones. A grave, a grave was what I had fallen into. I had been traversing what must have been the graveyard from the abandoned leper colony.

After this, there is really nothing to see as far as I am concerned. I go down to the beach and take the boat back to Y.

　　　　　　　　　　　　　　　　　　　　

That's not how it goes when I'm dreaming about it. That's *never* how it goes when I am dreaming about it. Want to know the rest? Nothing to it. You are no doubt thinking that in the dream, when I fall partially into the grave, my leg gets caught and I can't get out or something equally gothic.

No way. In this thing that's been pestering me all these years, I invariably get out of the grave alright, even get back to the beach alright, just as I did in life. But when I get back to the beach, I always find the boat is gone. There is no getting off this Hell.

Until I wake up.

Do you see all the gaps, friends? People on X and Y were unable to tell me enough to help me complete the picture. I have never blamed them though; they didn't have all the details or the wherewithal to help me anyway. They were unaware. Besides, in the end, I was the one who was supposed to be in charge of getting the facts. They are not at fault, that much I realize and accept.

If I could have got across to X(i) all would have been well, I am sure. If the people at Y had known more about Y(i) they would have told me about that stupid cemetery and I could have avoided it easily enough.

But there you are. People don't know enough, it seems. Imagine if they took more responsibility for knowing about things, what good would flow as a consequence.

But to the Committee, I say this—you were fully cognizant of the fact that I would only ever be able to glean part of the story in these places. I think you probably also knew about these offshore Islands, and deliberately chose not to tell me about them, because you were only interested in using me to get what you wanted.

It's what *you* want really. You dress it up and talk about Our Experience, Our Culture, and how we have to record it and measure it and chart it and understand and all that bullshit. But it's all simply to do with your own aggrandizement.

In addition to being corrupt you know, I was an innocent idiot who thought knowledge mattered. What a laugh! Of course it doesn't matter when it is controlled by people like you.

Know what I intend doing? I'm going to give it all away. I'm going to resign from any further duties of this sort. I have some money, you know. Money which I intend to spend on buying a boat, something big enough to take me to any Island anywhere. I'm going to get in this boat, fill it full of provisions and things to write with and on, and then sail off.

My first destination will be X(i), because that one is really quite close. There, I will do it all over again, I will do the job property—I will find out everything. I will get all the facts first hand and I will set them down. But for my benefit only, just mine, and nobody else's.

Unless there are other people I might discover in my travels who genuinely want to know. I will gladly share my knowledge with such people.

Later, of course, I will have to do the same at Y(i). This is the only way I can see by which I might lift the curse of these Islands. Nightmares, I sincerely believe, will become things of the past.

The only thing that's worrying me is this—I know there are many small Islands in the seas of the earth. I'm not sure I will ever be able to get to them all. I suppose the only thing one can do is try. I fervently hope that these Islands exist as single entities. Islands with Islands of their own, I have found, are very difficult to do.

ACKNOWLEDGMENTS

Some of these stories have been published before, sometimes in slightly different forms: 'Being Here Now' and 'Velodrome' in the *Bulletin*; 'I Told Mama Not to Come' in *The State of the Art*, edited by Frank Moorhouse (Melbourne: Penguin, 1983); 'Single Lens Reflex' in *Compass*.

The author wishes to acknowledge the assistance of the Literature Board of the Australia Council during the writing of this book.

ABOUT THE AUTHOR

Angelo Loukakis was born and educated in Sydney, where he still lives. His short stories and articles have been widely published in Australian journals, anthologies, and literary magazines, and his first collection of stories, *For the Patriarch*, was highly praised. He is the recipient of a Writer's Fellowship from the Literature Board of the Australia Council and is currently writing full-time.

COPYRIGHT

ligature *in*tapped

www.ingramcontent.com/pod-product-compliance
Lightning Source LLC
Chambersburg PA
CBHW030917060726
47591CB00005B/1583